John Leatherman
D0425785

BRIGHT DANGER

HUGH MACNAIR KAHLER

Bright Danger

TRIANGLE BOOKS

TRIANGLE BOOKS

New York

TRIANGLE BOOKS EDITION PUBLISHED DECEMBER, 1942

TRIANGLE BOOKS, 14 West Forty-ninth Street
New York, N. Y.

PRINTED IN THE UNITED STATES OF AMERICA
AMERICAN BOOK–STRATFORD PRESS, INC., NEW YORK

For

Bill and Billie Brann

BRIGHT DANGER

I

THE CLERK at the Beauregard-McGee was dapper and brisk and a little prissy. He leaned across the desk to shake hands with Rick. He shook hands, afterwards, with Dusty, but not so eagerly, and he kept on looking at Rick while he was doing it.

That suited Dusty. Being with Rick always made him feel like the Invisible Man in the trick movie, and he liked the feeling. If he'd been by himself he'd have been uncomfortable, walking across the big lobby with a flock of bellhops carrying the red-striped bags and everybody staring. As it was he almost liked the stares. They were all for Rick, and a guy like Rick ought to be stared at. It was one of the things he rated, like the toadying handshake from the clerk.

Dusty didn't rate it and didn't want to rate it. Being invisible made the dim, high-ceiled lobby feel restful to him.

He liked the Beauregard-McGee better than any of the other hotels he and Rick had stayed in, just as he liked Beauport best of all the oil towns. There were two Beauports, an old one, built lazily with cotton money, and a new one, sprouting up through it, that oil money had wanted, as it wanted everything, in a sweating hurry. And the Beauregard-McGee was two hotels, an old one, sprawling drowsily over half a block, and a new one, a slim spike of skyscraper, sticking up beside it, ten stories higher.

Dusty liked the old town and the old hotel better than the new ones. He liked the old Beauregard lobby, all marble and onyx and black walnut and gilt and plush; and he wasn't in any hurry to get over into the chromium and air-conditioned newness of the McGee.

The clerk's voice had butter on it as he held out the pen for Rick to register.

"We're full up, Mr. Farren, but I saved a suite for you in the new wing."

His eye slid past Rick toward the elevator-shaft, a big, old-fashioned one, walled in with gilded iron scroll-work. A fox-faced fat man and a woman with a sour mouth were just getting into one of the cars, with four bellhops carrying a lot of important-looking baggage. The man had a shivering little spider of a Mexican hairless dog on a leash and the woman was carrying a square leather box that Dusty guessed would have her spare jewelry inside of it. She had plenty of it on her. Halfway across the lobby Dusty could see her rings. One of them shot out a flash like the beam of a purple searchlight.

Dusty got a kick out of watching those two going up to stuffy rooms in the old wing. They wouldn't be doing it, he knew, if the clerk had been saving up that air-conditioned suite for anybody but Rick Farren.

That was the way it ought to be, Dusty thought. Rick ought to get things that the lousy-rich couldn't buy. Not that Rick wouldn't be buying the made-to-order weather in that suite, of course. Not that he wouldn't be paying more for it than the fox-faced man would have paid. Rick wasn't asking the clerk what it was going to cost. The fox-faced man would have asked.

Dusty got a kick out of that, too. Being teamed up with Rick had just about cured him of his Vermont ideas about money. Rick had made him see that all money was good for, or ever could be good for, was to spend. It wasn't any use to the people who tried to cuddle it. All they got out of it was the worry of trying to find a safe place to hide it and the everlasting fear that they'd be robbed of a piece of it. Even when they spent it, all they bought was headaches, like that sour-faced woman's box of diamonds and the dinky dog that looked like a bug. Even when they bought good times with it they headached over counting their change and trying to get six cents' worth of fun out of every nickel.

The clerk was talking again. "There've been a number of telephone calls for you, and Mr. Rogan" —he said the name as if it tasted holy to him—

"was here just a moment ago, asking for you, and he seemed surprised that you weren't already registered."

Dusty wondered about that. It was Dan Rogan's business to know pretty nearly everything, but he didn't see how even Rogan could have found out that they were heading this way. Rick hadn't thought of coming to Beauport till Stella telephoned him, and she hadn't telephoned till just before they started.

Rick seemed to be wondering about it too. He had on the dead-pan look that meant he was trying to figure something out and didn't expect to like the answer when he found it.

"There's Mr. Rogan now," the clerk said. There was a sort of hush in his voice. He nodded toward the doorway of the cocktail lounge that had once been a bar. To Dusty the air seemed to get a little cooler as Rogan came toward the desk. In white linen that didn't show a wrinkle he looked as if he'd been in cold storage. There was no color in his face, square-chinned, raked with lines around a mouth like a button hole. His eyes were colorless, too, and deep set under black brows, and they had the look that grows into a man's eyes when he spends twenty years in getting exactly what he wants and kicking other men in the belly to do it. Rogan didn't do his kicking in person any more, but Dusty guessed he could still do it, given a need or shown a profit. He still had the build of a middle-weight boxer, compact, neatly rugged.

He ignored Dusty but took a small smile off the ice for Rick.

"Nice work, Farren. I thought that Rio Seco fire was going to be tough, but McGoorty says you made it look easy."

"They all look alike to me and Duss." Rick didn't warm up. He never tried to cover up the way he felt about Rogan.

"If that's so, maybe I'd better knock a little off my price for the Bayou Rouge job." Rogan laughed. He must keep that laugh in the ice-box, too, when he wasn't using it, Dusty thought. "I won't, though. How would fifteen thousand sound to you?"

"I wouldn't know. I don't even hear it," Rick said. His voice had a saw-edge. Dusty knew why. Even if putting out oilwell fires was your regular business, it always made you sore when Dan Rogan talked as if it wasn't any different from the kind of business he did, safe and comfortable and cool, behind the big glass-topped desk in World Pete's air-conditioned office.

"Well, any time your hearing's better, let me know." Rogan's smile dipped downwards at the corners and his eyes, under the black eyebrows, were like two dimes. Dusty could guess how he and Rick must look to those eyes, how anybody must look to them who didn't jump at a chance to make money, any way he could, any time he could, whether he needed it or not. The two dimes weren't looking at Rick, though. They were going past him, toward somebody else. Big Jim Hafey, heading for the bar, a hulk of a man, sweating through his faded blue shirt, looked as if he must be having another run of rotten luck. He looked, too, as if he didn't like Dan Rogan any better than Rick did: his smooth, bricky face went hard and ugly as he turned it, for a second, toward the desk, and he walked on, a little quicker, as if seeing Rogan had made him more in a hurry to get his drink.

Rogan made a clicking noise with his tongue and teeth.

"Too bad. Hafey's up against enough trouble without putting a hangover on top of it. He's lost everything but his drilling rig and I guess he's lost that by now."

He made the clicking noise again.

"How'd he lose it?" Dusty asked. He liked Hafey. Hafey was one of the old-timers; he'd come up the hard way, from roustabout to driller and contractor; he'd struck it rich and gone broke again half a dozen times, and neither ups nor downs had made him anything but what he'd been to start with —an old-fashioned oil man, hard-fisted, square-shooting, heavy-drinking; rough, tough and durable, a friend to everybody but himself.

"Oh, he got mixed up with Frank Morel," Rogan said. "You know. The wild-catter who put down those three dry holes up at Saragossa. Hafey's been putting down another well for him and I hear he traded his rig for stock in Morel's company. If that's so he's all washed up. Even if there was a pint of oil under that country—and there isn't—they'll never get down to it. They're working on a shoestring and I don't believe there's much stretch left in it. I'm sorry. Hafey's never had any use for me but I've always liked the old rooster and I'll hate to see him down and out."

"Yeah," Rick said. "I can see it's just breaking your big heart. I'd let you cry on my shoulder only I've got work to do. Come on, Duss."

He swung away. As they passed the doorway of the bar Hafey came out. His face was still ugly but it brightened a little when Rick hailed him.

"Hello, boys." He included Dusty in his nod. "Come on in and have a shot with me. You must be needing one, after being that close to Dan Rogan."

"Give us rain-checks," Rick said. "In kind of a hurry, now. What's Rogan been doing to you this time?"

"Nothing," Hafey said. "He knows better than to try anything on me." He glanced toward the desk and his face went uglier than ever. "But he's making a nice try at putting something over on Frank Morel."

"Your partner, huh?" Rick said.

"Well, kind of. I got an interest in his wildcat up at Saragossa, but Morel's boss—or he was, till he took a nose dive off the rig and smashed a hip and a couple of ribs. Since then he's been up in a hospital in St. Louis having a swell time in a cast, and his kid's the boss. That'd be all right with me. Jan's an ace and we'd get along swell, if I could just figure out how to keep Rogan away from her till Frank can do his own watchdogging."

Rick laughed.

"I hope you get in a couple of bites while you're doing it," he said. "Take an extra one for me, will you?"

He led the parade of bellhops over to the arch that opened into the new wing. The wall of the corridor was plain and bare; the elevator doors were flat-finished chromium, instead of gilded iron. Dusty didn't feel comfortable, usually, in this kind of newness, but he was glad to get away from Dan Rogan. The suite was a corner one, high up, with furniture made out of bent pipes, but the dry, cool, conditioned air felt good, after the sticky heat downstairs.

Dusty let himself drop into the surprising comfortableness of one of the trick chairs. He watched Rick tipping the bellhops, overdoing it, the same as always. Fifty cents apiece to these boys didn't buy you anything, Rick said, but a couple of bucks to each of them and a five-spot to the captain gave them enough of a kick to put a kick in it for you. Dusty got one out of it this time, although the boys weren't thanking him and didn't even see him as they went out, happy and excited.

He leaned back and shut his eyes. That was a mistake. The Rio Seco fire was still printed on the back of his eyeballs, like the filament of a light-bulb that he'd been looking at too long. The second he let his eyelids come down he was staring at a blinding spike of flame, stabbing up into a cloud of soupy smoke. And that brought back a lot of other things he didn't want to think about. Wading through hot slushy mud. Breathing air that put blisters on his lungs. Sweat, running down his legs and making puddles in his shoes.

He heard Rick calling the bar and ordering two rum collinses. He watched Rick opening his bags and putting up suits on hangers. It was always a wonder to him, the way Rick could do things so fast and yet never seem to hurry. Rick left out the white gabardine. Dusty felt a little tireder when he saw that. It meant he'd have to change, too, from the skin up, and he didn't want to. It didn't occur to him, though, to give Rick an argument about it. The less a thing mattered the more set Rick was on having it his way.

"Snap out of it, will you, Duss?" Rick's voice was a little impatient. "We're going places."

Dusty got up and opened his biggest bag. By the time he'd changed into the white suit he felt a little better about it. There was a kind of lift in it. Standing in front of the long glass in the bathroom door he caught himself looking almost cheerful. But he stopped looking that way when the telephone buzzed and Rick answered it.

"Hi, Stel!"

Rick sounded excited. Dusty scowled. He'd known it was going to happen but that didn't make him like it. He was sick of always having to celebrate, after dousing a fire, in some town where Stella Conway happened to be peddling her line of beauty specialties. He didn't like Stella and he hated Rick's liking her.

It struck him, too, that if Dan Rogan had found out that Stella was in Beauport there wasn't any great mystery about his having guessed that Rick would be heading this way.

"Huh? Whadduyuh mean, blisters? Duss and I don't go that near 'em any more. They lay down when they see us starting."

Rick always talked like that. He wasn't gagging, either. It was the way he felt. As if an oil fire was nothing but a big four-flushing blowhard, that anybody could walk up to and slap down. Dusty had an idea that this might be one reason why they'd licked so many.

"Sixteen-double-o. Step on it, baby. Dusty can hardly wait."

He hung up, and turned, grinning.

"Stel's coming right up."

"That's a break." Dusty didn't even try to sound as if he meant it. Rick's grin rubbed itself out.

"What's back of that crack?" He didn't often use the sawtooth voice and the deadpan look on Dusty, but he was doing it now. Dusty was too tired to stall.

"I just can't make it add up, Rick. If I can spot Stella for a gold-digger it's a cinch she isn't fooling you. She doesn't even take the trouble to put on a good act. And——"

He stopped. Rick was looking just the way he looked when he sized up a fire. Then, suddenly, the grin came back.

"See if it'll add up this way, Duss. Any time I'm sitting in a crooked game, I like to know it's crooked. If I can't help seeing 'em switch decks I don't go betting too heavy on what they deal me. Well, in my book any game with a dame in it is strictly on the crook, see? If I'm going to sit in any, I'll pick one where there's no danger of me forgetting that they're dealing seconds on me. With Stel I couldn't forget it if I tried."

"And still it won't add up," Dusty said. "What's the use of sitting in at all, when you know the game's crooked?"

Rick's laugh was a little flat and tight.

"You know what the cowpunch said when they

asked him that one. 'Sure it's crooked, but it's the only game in town.' Do we let it go at that, huh?"

"Okay," Dusty said. It still didn't make sense, though. And when Rick opened the door, and Stella followed the waiter into the room, it made less sense than ever.

You only needed one eyeful of her, Dusty thought, to see that she was as cold as dry ice and hard as a keg of nails. She didn't try to keep you from seeing it. Her smile wasn't even pretending to be real, any more than the hard brightness of her ash-blonde hair. Even the lovely, long, flat slimness of her looked as it if would be hard, if you touched it, and cold.

It was no wonder, though, that she was selling beauty creams and lipsticks and nail lacquers to half the department stores in East Texas. She was a sort of living showcase for them.

She didn't even look at Dusty. She just twiddled her fingers at him as she went past him to the chair by the window. The light blinked on the emerald Rick had bought for her after the Tulsa job. Dusty didn't grudge her the money cost of it, although some of the money had been his. What he grudged her was being able to prove that she could play Rick Farren for a sucker. He didn't have to wait long to find out that she was going to keep on proving that.

She sat on the arm of the chair and shook her head when Rick offered her Dusty's drink.

"No, thanks. I can only stay a minute. I want to get down to Guldenberg's before they close. They're holding a wrist-watch for me. You wouldn't feel like tagging along, would you?"

"Why wouldn't I?" Rick said. "That's what I'm here for, isn't it? I hope you didn't forget to fix it up with Guldenberg so you get your cut."

"Is that nice?" Stella laughed. She slid off the chair and slipped a hand under Rick's sleeve. "Don't come, unless you want to."

Rick put down his glass. He gave Dusty a sidelong look, half grinning, as if he saw himself just the way Dusty was seeing him, and was getting a laugh out of it, too.

"What do you say, Duss? Do we go?"

Dusty was tempted, for a minute, to make up an excuse for not going. He was pretty tired, and he knew it would make him tireder to watch Stella making a fool of Rick. But just as he was going to tell them to go along without him he happened to catch Stella's eye, and it told him that she was hoping he wouldn't come. That made up his mind for him.

"Oh, all right," he said. Stella's disappointed look would have made it worth while, even without Rick's pleased grin. They rode down in one of the chromium elevators and came out into sudden, suffocating heat. It was a little cooler, though, in the jewelry store around the corner. Guldenberg waited on Stella himself, elbowing a clerk out of the way to do it. He was a small man, with a stripe of naked scalp; if he'd been a dog, Dusty thought, he'd have been wagging his tail.

He got the wrist-watch out of a drawer in the wall-safe behind him. He held it gingerly, almost as if it burned his fingers. Stella tried it on, holding her arm away from her and leaning her head back, with her eyes almost shut.

"Can't you possibly shade the price a little, Mr. Guldenberg?" Her voice was wheedling, creamy. "Four hundred's a lot of money."

Guldenberg shook his head sorrowfully.

"Not for this watch, Miss Conway. At seven-fifty it would be cheap. Only because an old customer must raise cash in a hurry could I make you such a price."

Stella kept on turning her wrist, this way and that.

"Want it, Stel?" Rick said.

"Oh, no," Stella said. "Not much. I wouldn't commit more than one murder for it, I guess."

She started to unhook the clasp. Rick reached out and stopped her.

"Keep it on," he said. He peeled four hundred-dollar bills off his roll and flipped them on the showcase. Guldenberg was reaching for them when Stella put her hand on them.

"Wait," she said. "It's a lovely watch and I'm crazy to have it, but it's not worth that much."

Guldenberg looked worried, but not quite worried enough, Dusty thought.

"I'll tell you what," Stella said, as if the idea had just struck her. "You give me a trial order for my perfumes and we'll buy the watch at your price.

That's only fair, isn't it? Say about two dozen, assorted, in the new crystal flasks."

Guldenberg pretended to think it over, but even Dusty could see it was only pretending. They'd had it all fixed up between them in advance. It was just a way for Stella to get her cut. He watched Rick while Stella made out the order and Guldenberg signed it; they weren't fooling Rick any, Dusty saw. He knew he was being trimmed. But he acted as if he liked it.

"A hundred and eight dollars," Stella said. "I'll make it an even hundred, cash."

She picked up one of the bills without waiting for Guldenberg to answer, and folded it carefully so as to fit into her compact; she gave Guldenberg a slow smile and took her time about walking to the door. Rick caught Dusty's eye.

"What's the matter, Duss? Still trying to make it add up?"

"No," Dusty said. "I guess it adds up all right—as long as it's the only game in town."

For a second, watching Rick's face, he was sorry he'd said it, and almost sorry for Rick himself. He didn't like that feeling. Nobody ought to be sorry for Rick. He was glad when Rick laughed and turned to follow Stella out.

They went back to the Beauregard-McGee. The new cocktail lounge was cool and the bent-pipe chairs in it were comfortable. Dusty took it easy in one of them, watching Stella and Rick playing a slot-machine. You had to hand it to Stella, he told himself. Nobody else had ever figured out a way to beat the slot-machines, but Stella had a system that couldn't lose. She just let Rick feed in the half-dollars while she collected any that came out.

Old Jim Hafey was over on the far side of the room, sitting by himself. He had two or three drinks while Dusty watched him and when he got up and went out Dusty could see that he'd already had plenty of others. Dusty didn't blame him much. Any man, he guessed, would be apt to do a little elbow-bending if he had to take orders from a girl and try, at the same time, to keep Dan Rogan away from her.

Maybe it was because Jim Hafey had called her an ace; maybe it was because, according to Jim, Dan Rogan was making a play for her; maybe it was because she was up against a job that had licked plenty of good men. Without knowing why he felt that way about a girl he'd never seen and hardly heard of, Dusty was interested in her, and curious about her, and on her side.

2

JAN MOREL had started on the long drive out from Beauport with a cargo of assorted worries, but some of them had managed to get lost along the way.

It was always like this on her trips out to the lease. Just turning the battered muzzle of the old Pierce Arrow toward Saragossa was like the beginning of an escape from troubles that somehow couldn't seem to follow her out into the flat, empty countryside of scrubby timber and scattered cotton fields.

She kept on worrying about her father, to be sure.

There wasn't any escape from that anxiousness. But she could almost forget about the pile of envelopes on her desk that she hadn't dared to open, envelopes with those ugly transparent mouths that always seemed to be trying to show their teeth. She could push into the back of her mind the regretful head-shake with which friendly Tom Harrod, at the bank, had turned down her plea for another loan. She could push into the back of her mind the warning from the tax collector. Out here, getting nearer and nearer to the place where the drill was probing for it, she could almost manage to believe that there was really oil down there, and that this time the drill was going to find it.

Back in Beauport it was harder to believe that. Back there you didn't see men working their heads off to drill down to where the oil ought to be. You only heard men talking, and all the talk was what you didn't want to hear, and the ones who said the most were most discouraging of all. Tom Harrod, for instance, claiming he was doing you a favor by not letting you borrow another dime to drop down another dry hole. Even Dan Rogan, who had hired the best geologists in the business to seismograph the Saragossa territory for World Pete, urging you to quit and cut your losses.

But out here, always, you could somehow manage to believe you were going to win. To hope so, anyway. Out here, where things were happening, you could get back your faith in old Jim Hafey and convince yourself that Dan Rogan's high-priced rock-hounds were all wrong.

Always, when you turned off the concrete and slowed for the bumpy dirt road that twisted through the scrub, you watched the skyline ahead of you with a queer small tingle of excited eagerness.

The same kind of eagerness, Jan told herself impatiently, with which a poker-player reaches for a new hand or a crap-shooter waits for the dice to stop rolling.

It always angered her a little to find that there was this much of the gambler in her. She wanted to believe there wasn't any. She had no use for the stupid business of taking needless chances. What she had hated worst about her father's oil adventures hadn't been their costly unluckiness but the fact that every one of them had been a gamble, a blind gamble against crazy odds. She tried her best to think that she would have hated them just as hard if they had won. And catching herself in the act of feeling differently toward this final one, just because it still stood a chance of winning, was a shaming proof that she wasn't quite free, after all, from the same folly she intelligently scorned in other people.

And yet the eagerness quickened as she neared the lease. She didn't lose it till she was driving over the plank road through the last stretch of swampy woodland and caught sight of the steel spider-web of derrick above the tree-tops.

There were a lot of thribbles—she had learned to think of those triple, ninety-foot stands of drill-pipe by the name the drillers gave them—racked inside of that derrick, and little as she knew about her job, she knew enough to be quite certain that they meant grief.

They hadn't been there, yesterday, when she had started for town. She couldn't think of any reason for their being there now that didn't promise trouble for her. She stopped her car beside the slab tool-house and hurried over to the rig.

For all her anxiety she couldn't help feeling the

little thrill she always got out of watching the drilling crew at this part of their business. Pulling that mile of drill-pipe out of the well was using up time she couldn't spare and costing money she couldn't afford, but there was a kick in seeing it happen.

Always, watching it, Jan felt a sort of poetry in the rhythm of it, the varied roar of the Diesels, the fierce downward swoop of the elevators to clamp their jaws on the top of that mile of hanging steel, the beautiful symphony of strength and skill in the timed bend and sweep with which the two men lifted out the heavy steel wedges—slips they called them—that had been holding the hanging pipe in place, and lifted them back when ninety feet of it had come up out of the hole; the effortless, perfectly timed swings of the giant tong that unscrewed it; the derrick-man, reaching out from his eagle's perch to free the elevators for another plunge. There was a kind of wonder in this magic partnering of flesh and blood against the gods, against the obstinate perversity of the inanimate, multiplying with every inch of added depth, the sulking, stubborn malice of mere heaviness, the sullen, passive enmity of rock, the trickiness of sand and water, the giant pressures, raging in their prison, biding their time.

It always stirred Jan's blood and warmed it. She had learned respect and something like affection for the men who matched themselves against those gods —men self-selected for savage strength, savage endurance of toil and hardship, savage indifference to pain and joy in danger, savage contempt of death. Thinking of them she always remembered words written about the conquest of another frontier— "the cowards never started and the weak died on the way."

The phrase was in her mind as she climbed to the derrick floor. Ivan Gary and Odd Shape Pender, the two men at the slips and Guthead Marr, the tool-pusher, were tough and rough—in their language the word roughneck was an honorable title, hard-won, distinguishing them from lesser men who had still to earn it—but there was nothing of the weakling or the coward in any of the three.

"What's the idea?" She had to shout to make herself heard above the engines.

"Hafey's orders." Guthead didn't take his eyes off

their business. "He says we got to put on a new bit."

There wasn't anything to say to that. Jim Hafey knew what he was doing and he was in command. But something in the quality of Guthead's bellow told Jan he wasn't pleased.

She wasn't pleased, either. A new bit cost ninety dollars, besides the lost time, and there was no credit, any more, at any of the supply houses. Another ninety feet of pipe clanged against the rack. She caught Guthead's sleeve as the elevators came down.

"Wait, Guthead. We're not changing bits. This one's got to get us down to oil or we don't get there."

Guthead turned his head a second. Under the grease there was a queer look in his weatherbitten face.

"I'm working for Hafey," he shouted. "I do what he says and he says to pull her." The elevators started up again, the noise rising with it. Guthead leaned close to Jan, cupping his hand to shut his voice in for her ear. "Relax. You won't need no new bit."

He winked at her, a sly, droll wink, and his teeth showed white as a dog's in the grin that split his face. He jerked his head toward the doghouse and Jan went over to it and waited. She felt better. She couldn't imagine what Guthead had to tell her that he didn't want the rest of the crew to overhear, but she knew it wasn't anything for her to worry about. After a while he came to the door of the shack.

"I tried to tell Hafey you was too wise to go for that bedtime story about having to change bits, but he said to hand it to you, so I done it. But I ain't got no orders not to slip you my private hunch, and I figure you got it coming to you. The next thing down that hole is gonna be a swab."

Jan knew what that meant. A swab lifted the liquid mud out of a well to let gas and oil come into the bottom of it. Jim Hafey wouldn't be getting ready to swab unless he was pretty sure the oil was there.

"We're on the sand, then! Why didn't Mr. Hafey want me to know?"

Guthead shrugged his bull shoulders.

"It might not mean a thing. Guess Hafey figures you've had about all you can take and don't want to get you all lit up over what might be nothing but a false alarm. Me, I got you sized up different. Anyhow, I'm telling you."

Jan kept still. She hadn't known how much it mattered. Sometimes, when she'd thought about striking oil, she'd imagined that she'd be up on top of the world, and it was a queer, dull shock to find that she wasn't. All she could feel was a sort of let-down. As if something had been winding up her nerves like banjo-strings and suddenly, just when they were going to snap, had let them go loose.

"What's the matter with me, Guthead? I'm not even glad. I'm just tired."

"Sure," he said. "You been gambling, and you ain't a gambler."

She nodded slowly.

"Yes. That's right. All I ever wanted was the chance to quit."

"I know," Guthead said. "That's why I stuck my neck out, tipping you off."

"What do you mean?" Jan spoke sharply. "How are you sticking your neck out by telling me anything there is to tell about this job? You're working for me."

He wagged his head.

"No. Hafey's working for you. Me, I work for

him. And he don't hire me to do his talking for him. I stuck my neck out, all right, telling you, if you leave him know I done it."

"But that's nonsense. He'd have told me himself if——"

"If he'd wanted you told," Guthead said.

"But why wouldn't he want me to know?" Jan was angry and puzzled. She liked Jim Hafey and trusted him and she resented the dim doubt of him that Guthead's talk was putting into her mind. She was trying not to ask herself why, with good news for her at last, he had kept it to himself.

"He might have his reasons," Guthead said, "and they might be good ones. I could make a guess at one of 'em, maybe."

"What?" Jan said.

"Well, you ast for it, so don't get sore at me for handing it to you," he said defensively. "Hafey might be figuring you'd put Dan Rogan wise."

"What if I did?" Jan kept a tight grip on her temper but it wasn't easy. It was bad enough to put up with unreasonable disapproval from her father and Jim Hafey of her perfectly harmless friendliness with Dan Rogan, without having to take it from Guthead, too. "Jim Hafey doesn't expect to keep it a secret, does he, if we strike oil?"

"He ain't in no hurry for Rogan to know we're getting close to it, anyhow," Guthead said. "I ain't figured out why, but I'm plenty sure it's so. Yesterday, when Rogan sent McGoorty out here snooping for him, Hafey hustled in the shack and hid them last cores we taken, and when he let McGoorty look over the others he told him that was all there was. He don't want Rogan to know any quicker than he has to. So I'm asking you to keep it under your hat till he tells you himself. I figure you owe me that much for tipping you off."

"It doesn't make sense," Jan said, "but I'll do it. If there's only some oil down there, nothing else matters. But——"

She stopped. Guthead had stiffened suddenly, listening. She heard a queer, deeptoned rumbling sound, far down in the earth.

"She's blowing out!" Guthead said. He started running and Jan ran with him till a sweep of his arm sent her stumbling backward.

"You stay the hell outa this! She might catch fire."

The arm convinced her. She might have disobeyed the words. The rumble was swelling up into a vast bubbling roar. Up through the frame of the derrick a great spout of black mud shot into the air, tossing the last few sections of the drill-stem like so many straws. Jan wasn't frightened till she saw, mingling with the blackness of the mud and oil, the steamy whiteness that meant gas. She knew what would happen if one of the thousands of rock fragments flying up through the derrick should strike a hot spark on the steel of it. She saw men running and wondered why the blowout-preventer hadn't been closed. And then, over the derrick, like a balloon misshapen by a wind, a distorted globe of fire.

There was a noise like the sound of a flock of giant geese taking wing. Great mushroom-like clusters of flame went rolling upward, fiery umbrellas, burning outward from their centers and exploding. And suddenly, striking Jan's face like a blow, heat, a searing gale of heat. And the world was filled with sound, a maniac, shrieking fury of it, intolerable. Jan's hands tried uselessly to shut it out of her ears. There wasn't any power in her for thinking; her mind was paralyzed by the flame, the overwhelming sea of sound, the swift disintegration of the steel derrick like a spider's web in the blast of a blow-torch. She was dwarfed, an ant, under the careless, spurning foot of something too immense for her ant's senses to measure, her ant's intelligence to conceive.

Under that brain-numbing realization of littleness and impotency, she could not even be afraid.

The thing that sent her running—it did not seem to be swift movement, but the creeping, ridiculous and futile, of an inchworm—was not fear, but only the reflex action of nerves that shrank away from searing heat, and muscles that obeyed them blindly. Something had happened to the fire; it had suddenly changed shape; it wasn't a towering flame, now, but a twisted, flattened mushroom; the ragged fringe of it shot out toward her; she saw puddles explode into steam, saw the stumps of trees and the planks of the road leap into incandescence, the shacks blaze up and melt.

Turning, she ran again, till the heat on her back was bearable. There was a queer comfort in coming to her car; it was something homely and familiar, something infinitely small, like her, and yet, like her, surviving. She flung herself to the friendliness of the worn leather seat; unbidden her hands and feet found starter and gear-lever; the car carried her backward into safety that she did not recognize, at first, as safety, but only as a return, like the escape from a nightmare, to reality and consciousness and sanity.

She could think again. She could listen, understandingly, to Guthead's voice, with no knowledge of how he came to be beside the car. He was cursing somebody with a prayerful earnestness that lent a kind of sanctity to short, salty words. Unshocked, she sifted meaning from them.

It was Hafey's fault for saving pennies, buying junk. The blowout-preventer hadn't worked; it was wrecked, now, and the casing under it must have split. That was what was shooting the fire out flatly. The wreckage of the rig had helped, maybe. It was a cockeyed miracle the crew were all alive.

"It's a——" Guthead put together three words that in any other connection would have shocked Jan's ear.

"How do we put it out?" Her mind was clear again, and at work.

"We don't. We'd stand more show of dousing hell by——" Again a figure of speech, earthily elemental, slid past Jan without offense. "We hire Rick Farren and Duss Miller. Nobody else is crazy enough to stand a chance of getting by with it. But we get one break. Farren and Miller are over at Beauport, and by now they ought to be about ready for another piece of money. We——"

Jan laughed. She knew about Farren and Miller.

"And how do they get it out of us? Every cent we could get our hands on is down in that hole. And Farren and Miller don't do business on credit, do they? I've always heard they want plenty and they want it in cash."

"Yeah. But that don't mean you couldn't handle 'em. Rick Farren's a sucker for a gamble, and he ain't so strong-minded, neither, about the dames. I wouldn't put it past him to fall for a sporting proposition, like taking a piece of the lease, say, not if it was you that put it up to him." His eyes, looking out through holes in the mask of grease and soot, surveyed her critically. "Not if you scraped some of the tar off your pan and got inside of a few she-clothes. You got what it takes. Why, listen, there's even been times when I could pretty near of went for you myself."

He said it so seriously that Jan couldn't laugh. She didn't even find it funny. Instead, better than anything else he could have said, it gave her confidence in herself and a kind of faith in his idea.

"Here's what you do. You beat it to town, and take time when you get there to pretty up. Maybe you can locate Hafey, and maybe he'll be some use to you if you find him, but I'd hate to bet on it. He looked to me like he had another swell souse coming on, so don't take too long hunting for him. Go after Rick and Duss. They might be at the Beauregard, but it'll be night before you get there, and the chances are you'll have to dig 'em out of some hot spot. The Winter Garden, most likely. Look there first, anyhow. And get going."

Jan got going. She had to drive gingerly on the dirt road, washboarded, potholed and so narrow that it needed neat steering to pass the cars that were already heading toward the fire. One of them was driven by Tim McGoorty, and she laughed at herself because, as she went by him with a hurried wave and nod, she caught herself wondering why he should be out here again, and feeling, for a silly second, as if there might be something, after all, to that talk of Guthead's.

There couldn't be anything to it, of course. Dan Rogan might have sent McGoorty out here, yesterday, to look things over, but if he had he'd done it merely out of a natural, friendly interest in Jan Morel and her affairs. And McGoorty's being here again today didn't mean anything except that he'd been passing by, out on the highway, and had seen the smoke. She pushed the idea impatiently out of her mind. There were too many other things to think about.

It was ridiculous that she didn't seem to find anything fantastic about Guthead's idea of fighting an oil-well fire with such things as—there was even a sort of rightness in his choice of words—as some she-clothes and a pan with the tar scraped off it. Fire and sex were both very simple, elemental things.

Simple, elemental men like Guthead, dealing with one as simply as with the other, might very well know more about them than people who wrote books.

She decided that she'd wear the green organza. There'd be a kind of poetic justice if that last extravagance of hers should help her hypnotize Rick Farren into making it possible for her to pay for it.

3

DAN ROGAN took his smile out of cold-storage and spread it on his face. He put down the telephone and picked up another one. A private wire was only one of the many ways in which his left hand was kept in useful ignorance as to the operations of his right.

The office windows were blue-black with night before he had the answer he wanted. It did not please him when he heard it. The smile disappeared and he moved the receiver away from his ear; the voice that jostled out of it was loud and boisterously merry, slurring its consonants. Even over a wire it seemed to bring disorder into the clean room, disorder and the smell of stale smoke and sweat and whiskey. Rogan's own voice knifed delicately through it. He had his own technique for dealing with drunks.

"Good evening, Hafey. I'm sorry to disturb you at your innocent pleasures, but I thought it might interest you to hear that your wild-cat blew out this afternoon."

The exaggerated precision of his speech, the dry, quiet neutrality of his voice, had the effect he had learned to count on. Even over a wire they seemed to infect Hafey with some of their sobriety. There was less whiskey in his answer.

"Good God, Rogan——"

"Do you know, I think it might be better if you left my name out of your conversation?" Rogan kept to his key. "And perhaps you could lower your voice a little, too. I can hear you quite well, and there's no need for anybody at your end to hear you at all. Someone might find it singular that good news should seem to disappoint you——"

"Disappoint me hell!" Hafey's bellow wasn't quite

so loud, this time, but it was uglier than ever. "Listen, Rogan, if you——"

"Shut up!" Rogan hadn't lost any of his patience. He merely judged that it was time to change the treatment. "You'll have plenty of chances, later on, to explain why you've been keeping me in the dark and what you thought it would get you. Right now you've got something else to do. Your well's in, but it's afire—no, I'll do all the talking for the present—it's afire and McGoorty says it's going to stay that way for quite a while. He says the blowout-preventer's smashed and the casing's split below it, and the fire's shooting out almost flat for eighty or hundred feet all around it. He says it's pretty much like that headache of ours down at Bayou Rouge, only worse."

In spite of him a little cheerfulness squeezed into his voice.

"I'm afraid you'll have to postpone the rest of your bender, Hafey. It's going to take money to douse this fire and you've got to get busy and dig it up."

He chuckled.

"And you're going to have a sweet job doing it—such a sweet job that I wouldn't be surprised if some stock in your funny little company changed hands before you swung it. Maybe even enough to——" He left the sentence in the air and laughed again. Hafey was nearly sober now.

"By God, Rogan, if somebody plugged you in the guts you'd pull out the slug and make money on it."

"We haven't time for compliments," Rogan said. "You get out to that well. Have somebody else do the driving, though. Your head sobers sooner than your hands, I've noticed. It'll look better if you have a shot at the fire yourself below before you go out after the money to hire Rick Farren." He laughed again. "According to McGoorty, that idea has already occurred to Miss Morel. McGoorty says she's here in town now, looking for Farren." Another chuckle. "Just what she expects to use for money I don't know."

"She might get by without it," Hafey said.

"Don't make me laugh," Rogan said. "I offered Farren fifteen thousand, just this afternoon, to go after the Bayou Rouge job, and it didn't dent him.

He's off the market till he's through splitting his roll between Mink Schwartz's dice game and Stella Conway. Forget it, and get going."

He put down the receiver. After a moment, though, he lifted it again.

"Schwartz? Rick Farren there?" The smile came out of the icebox again. "That's fine. Listen. . . ."

4

THE FOUNTAIN ROOM in the new wing of the Beauregard-McGee was pleasantly cool, but Dusty didn't manage to get much comfort out of it. The band kept making a lot of hottish, restless-sounding noise, and so did the dinner-show. He didn't mind the three girls in dude-ranch clothes who crooned cowpunch songs in close harmony, but the rattle and clack of the tap-dance numbers seemed to be hammering on his brain, and a team of trick roller-skaters, doing their act on the top of a little iron table, were the worst of all.

His nerves were still edgy after the Rio Seco fire and he couldn't help ducking when the man skater did those whirligig spins, holding the girl by her legs so that her head kept whizzing past Dusty's, only a few feet away. Rick and Stella laughed at him for that, and he guessed they had a right to laugh at anybody who would eat dinner in a place like this, feeling the way he did about it.

Feeling that way was something new. Up to now he hadn't minded being wherever Rick wanted to be, even when he couldn't imagine why Rick should want to be there. If he didn't like what Rick liked it just proved that he didn't know enough to like the right things. But tonight he didn't seem to see it that way. Instead of wondering at himself for not being smart enough to have a good time here, he caught himself thinking that there was something pretty dumb about trying to have a good time this way, about coming to a place like this to try to have it.

He pushed the idea out of his head and felt ashamed of having let it in. But he kept on wishing he was somewhere else, and he was glad when Rick decided it was time to move on, although he knew he wasn't going to like it much better at any of the places where Rick and Stella would be apt to go.

Rick wanted to try the Winter Garden, for a starter, and see how the dice were rolling. Dusty didn't care for the place, but the hot stickiness of the night made him glad to get out of it again. Big Jim Hafey was leaning against the long chromium bar in the front room, when they came in, and he had got to the stage where anybody he knew had to drink with him or else. Dusty didn't mind doing it. The high, leather-topped stool was comfortable and so was the quietness, after the racket at the Fountain Room. His rickey was gratefully cool to the heel of his blistered hand, too, and the more time he spent out here the less he'd have to spend in the back room, watching Rick trying to outguess the dice. He was sorry when a waiter came and told Hafey he was wanted on the telephone and Rick jumped at the chance to make a getaway.

The telephone booths were in the corridor that led to the back room. Hafey was in one of them, shouting so that his voice came through the glass door. Stella stopped short and slipped into the other booth.

"I almost forgot. I've got to make a call myself."

She shut the door. Rick hesitated, scowling a little, but she gave him a smile through the glass, and waved her hand for him to go on without her, and after a moment he did. Dusty went with him.

The big room was almost empty, this early. The chuck-a-luck game had a couple of customers and three people were at one of the roulette tables. Dusty got a laugh out of two of them—the fox-faced man and the sour-mouthed woman he'd noticed at the hotel. It only needed one look to tell him that their money wasn't buying them much fun here.

Rick spotted them, too, and they handed him a laugh, Dusty could see. Rick usually couldn't be bothered with roulette, but he stopped, this time, and made a few careless bets, dropping five-dollar bills on single numbers. Dusty knew he was only doing it for the fun of watching those two strained faces. The same look was in them both—tightlipped, frowning, intent. They were playing a system. The man had a ruled pad in front of him and after every spin he'd do some quick, complicated bookkeeping on it and tell the woman, in a sharp undertone, how many chips to bet on the next roll, and her rings would glitter as she counted them out and pushed them, with a nervous little jabby motion, out on the board.

It didn't seem to give them much of a kick to win, but when they lost they hated it. Watching them gave Dusty back his old faith in Rick's rightness. Rick had lost fifty bucks or so while they'd been winning three or four, but every losing spin had been fun for Rick, and nothing that these two dollar-cuddlers could ever do with money would be any real fun for them.

Dusty couldn't help feeling a little sorry for them, but Rick wasn't sorry. He laughed under his breath as he moved over to the crap-game, and Dusty knew what he was laughing at. Nothing looked so funny to Rick as people trying to buy themselves a good time with money that it hurt them to let go of. Watching those two faces had keyed him up a little higher, made him feel how much smarter he was, given him an extra reason for getting a kick out of trying to beat Mink Schwartz's dice.

Whoever had educated those dice, Dusty told himself, had used his head. They knew enough not to be in a hurry. They rolled Rick's way almost as often as against him and his losing bets weren't much bigger than his winning ones. After he'd played for ten or fifteen minutes he was still almost even and beginning to get restless. There was never any kick for him in staying even, at any game he played. He kept looking toward the door and as soon as Stella came through it he turned his back to the table and stood watching her as she came across the room. She took her time about it. Dusty thought she must have heard good news over the telephone, judging by the way she looked. Rick seemed to think so, too, and not to like it. He had on his dead-pan look.

"You certainly got a big nickel's worth," he said. His voice sounded flat. Stella laughed.

"I didn't even spend a nickel, sugar. The line was busy. I've been having a talk with Mink Schwartz. Look at what he bought me."

She laughed again as she flourished a highball

glass, half empty. After a second Rick laughed, too.

"That sets a new record," he said. "Hurry up and drink it and we'll blow before he comes around with the check."

Stella shook her head. She pulled a high-stool toward her and climbed up on it.

"Let's don't blow," she said. "What's the use of my fixing it up with Mink to get my cut on what you lose if you won't give me a chance to collect? The dice won't like you any better anywhere else. You haven't got any license to be lucky with them. You're too lucky with—" she gave him another laugh—"with the women."

Rick's face froze up again. Dusty could see that Stella wasn't fooling him. He knew perfectly well that she was getting a cut from Mink Schwartz and only telling the truth about it as the best way of pretending that she wasn't. But it didn't seem to matter to him. After a second he grinned at her.

"Okay, baby."

He turned around to the table. There were more men playing, now, and one of them, although there was plenty of room on the other side of the table, had crowded in next to Rick, a thickset man, bull-necked and dishfaced. It looked to Dusty as if he were trying to get in Rick's hair. He kept elbowing him and reaching across in front of him, almost as if he knew that Rick was like a cat about hating to be touched and was pushing him around on purpose to start something.

But that didn't make sense. Nobody but a drunk would start anything with Rick, and the bull-neck was cold sober. Dusty edged a little closer, close enough, when Rick and the bull-neck both reached out for the same pile of winnings, to be within easy arm's length of them both.

"What's the idea?" Rick's voice was quiet. The bull-neck didn't seem to know what that meant, but Dusty knew. Out of the tail of his eye, too, he saw a man on the other side of the bull-neck shake an arm a little, as if there might be something up his sleeve.

"The idea's that you're trying to grab off my dough!" The voice, too, was like a bull's. "You cheap chiseler, I'll——"

Just in time, Dusty got a shoulder in front of Rick and one hand on the bull-neck's necktie. With the other he jerked down on the free end of the tie and pulled it tight.

"Hold it, brother." He didn't have any trouble about grinning. He was suddenly feeling cheerful again. "I'll call the bouncer for you." He swung the man around so that he blocked the man behind him. "He'll be right in, soon as I——" He put his thumb firmly on the bull-neck's nose—"soon as I push the button. See? Like this."

He heard Rick laugh as the skewed nose flattened out under his thumb, and he felt a little easier. Rick was the one he had to worry about. Bull-neck and his buddy weren't starting the real party—their play was to let Rick do that. It would look all right, then, when two or three more of them took a hand, and Rick happened to bump into a blackjack or bottle or a chair. Something like that was due to happen, Dusty guessed. Whoever was back of them, these two thugs were here to give Rick the works, and if anything started, they'd get plenty of chance to do it. When Rick went to town he went all the way. The lookout was edging around from the end of the table, one hand in a pocket. He was in on the play, too, Dusty guessed. He wasn't looking at Dusty or the bull-neck; he was watching Rick. That was the tip-off. In about ten seconds, even with Bull-neck out of it, one of the others would do something and Rick would stop laughing and——

There was a little tinkle of splintering glass at Dusty's elbow. Out of the corner of his eye he saw a hand, long and slim-fingered, with purple-painted nails. It was holding the heel of a highball glass; the light winked on the points and edges of the jagged top. The lookout froze to a point, like a bird-dog, and Bull-neck's mate stepped back, carefully, like somebody backing away from a snake. The cold feeling between Dusty's shoulderblades had thawed a little even before he heard Stella's voice.

"I do hope I don't forget there's a lady present."

Dusty caught himself almost liking Stella. The laugh that went up in back of him meant that whatever had been framed up wasn't coming off, and it was Stella who'd done the trick. His own play wouldn't have been enough. He felt surer about that when he saw the back door open and the bouncer standing in it, the shape of a boxcar, with Mink Schwartz peeping out under his elbow like a mouse under a bureau. Whatever they'd been waiting for, on the other side of the door, they hadn't been waiting for a laugh.

It only took Mink a second to pick his play. He ducked under the bouncer's arm and came in.

"What seems to be the trouble?" He had a small, chirpy voice that might have fooled anybody who didn't look at the mouth it came out of.

Dusty looked over his head at the bouncer. Another laugh wouldn't hurt anything.

"Why, hello, Elmer." He got the laugh. "This baby wants you. I was just ringing for you. Like this."

He pushed the button again, just hard enough to make it funny. He could see Schwartz deciding to get off the fence on the sunny side.

"Outside." Schwartz jerked his head toward the door. Dusty guessed it was all right to let go of the necktie. Bull-neck was a hired man, hearing from his boss. He didn't even make a bluff at putting up a squawk. He only loosened his tie and went out, with the bouncer's hand on his arm. His buddy went along, stepping carefully wide of Stella. Dusty got a grin out of that, too. Schwartz came over to the table.

"I'm sorry, Mr. Farren. It won't happen again."

"That takes a load off my mind, Mink," Stella said. She gave the little man a small smile, and tapped the broken highball glass lightly against a standing ashtray. Some new splinters tinkled down the hollow stem of the ashtray. The mouse-under-the-bureau look came back into Schwartz's face. It had a right to, Dusty thought. He kept on almost liking Stella. She was only playing her own game, of course, but there was something swell about the way she did it. Dusty wondered whether maybe he might be wrong about her, after all.

And then, all at once, he forgot she was alive.

He was looking past her, at another girl, a girl in a misty green dress, a girl with red hair and a bridge of freckles across her nose, showing through the powder.

A waiter was with her. He said something to her that turned her eyes toward Dusty. There wasn't any reason why that should have excited him. He was used to being pointed out and stared at. But it hadn't ever made him feel the way he felt when this red-haired girl looked at him.

She came straight toward him. Rick was watching her, his back to the table, his hands resting on it. She gave him a quick glance and stopped in front of Dusty.

"Mr. Farren?" Her voice sounded just the way Dusty had been expecting it to sound. He shook his head and motioned her toward Rick. She looked disappointed, he thought. He got another unreasonable kick out of that, and out of the difference in her voice when she used it on Rick.

"I'm Jan Morel, Mr. Farren."

Dusty straightened. It had been funny to think of Dan Rogan falling for a girl, when Jim Hafey had talked about it, but it wasn't funny now.

"Go on from there," Rick said.

"I've got a job for you."

"Where? Not on that Saragossa wild-cat?"

Her eyes went wide. That made them green, Dusty noticed, instead of gray. He didn't blame her for being surprised. There was no way for her to know that Rick's brain worked as fast as his muscles, and that he never forgot anything he heard.

"Why, yes. How did you know?"

"I get around," Rick said. "All you had to tell me was your name. I know the rest of it. I know you and old Jim Hafey have been wild-catting up at Saragossa on a shoestring and if you've got a job for me and Duss I know that's where it has to be. What I don't know is how you figure you can hire us. Or maybe your idea is for us to write the job on the cuff?"

Dusty wondered whether a girl could fake a blush. This one certainly looked real. A laugh went with it, and that sounded real, too.

"No. I know better than to hope for anything like that. My idea was to give you a piece of the lease. It——"

"Hold it." Rick made a stop-signal with one hand. "No dice."

"But, why? It's your business, isn't it, putting out fires?"

"Sure it's our business. We take a chance on getting cooked when we need a piece of sudden money, but we wait till we need it, see? And right now we don't need it."

"But I'm offering you a chance——"

"Yeah. A chance to play the lead in a French fry and take our pay in sucker-bait if we live to collect! A piece of a lease to put in a frame and hang on the wall. A——"

"A piece of a lease that will pay you more than you ever got for any other job! It's going to be worth——"

"Going to be. Where did I hear that one before? Listen, baby, Duss and I are suckers every other way there is but that's one sucker bet we never play. Blue sky is blue sky, net, in our book. All anything's worth to us is what it's worth this very now. Not tomorrow. In our racket we don't use tomorrows."

The girl turned and gave Dusty a slow, straight look. It got to him. Most girls made him feel dumb and thumbfingered. This one was different. She only made him feel like a heel. He pulled his eyes away from hers, but when she went on he could feel that she was talking to him, now, and not to Rick.

"Yes. And I'm giving you a chance to get out of it and into something where they do use tomorrows. You'd never need to go near another fire if you'd——"

Rick had been finishing his drink. He set down the glass.

"Save it, sister. You're Myrna Loy and you got a million in each mitt, and still it's no dice. Have it your own way and say we're lame-brains to turn you down. Okay. We're lame-brains. That's the kind it takes in our racket, and that's the kind we are, see?"

"Yes, I see." Jan's voice was different. It sounded to Dusty as if she was talking from the other side of a barrier or a pit, close and yet a long, long way off. "I see just what kind you are. I don't know how you ever managed to sell men like Jim Hafey and Guthead Marr the idea you're anything else. Sailors on a spree. Blanket Indians, blowing in your oil money on gold cuspidors for your dirt-floored shacks, kid roustabouts, pleased to death with yourselves for feeding your wages to crooked gamblers and a——" Her eyes went slowly from Stella's ash-blonde bob to the black and silver sandals with the rhinestone heels, and back again, past the emerald, to the diamond clip.

Stella laughed.

"Go on, dearie. Give him the rest of it. 'Crooked

gamblers and gold-digging blondes.' Go ahead. Don't be afraid you'll hurt my feelings."

Jan's face changed a little. Some of the iciness thawed out of it. She shook her head.

"I did start to say that, but I won't. I haven't anything against you except the company you keep."

"Ouch!" Rick said. Jan turned her eyes to him, slowly.

"I shouldn't have bothered you, Mr. Farren. I can see there wasn't any need to. If all it takes to put out oil-well fires is somebody like you, I can do it myself! And I'm going to."

She split a look between him and Dusty. This time Rick could have had all of it, as far as Dusty was concerned. It kept him feeling like a heel as he watched her walk out.

"Why the quick brush-off, Rick? The kid's on the spot, and——"

"It's her spot," Rick said. "She can have it."

"Her proposition looked good to me," Dusty said. "This might be our chance at important money. A piece of that lease could put us on the plush for life."

"He's down!" Stella imitated a radio announcer.

"They're counting over Dusty. One—two—three——"

"Skip the clowning." Rick never used that voice on Stella except when she took a crack at Dusty. It took some of the soreness out of Dusty to hear it. But Rick used it on him, too. "Important money, huh? When did we ever handle any other kind? What do you call this?" He pulled out what was left of the Rio Seco payoff. "If this kind isn't important enough, I know where to go get the kind that is. We don't have to go play hook-and-ladder for bright blue sky and a pat on the head from a streamlined jill—not with Rogan waving fifteen cash g's under our nose for the Bayou Rouge job!"

Rogan. There was a sort of click in the back of Dusty's head, as if something was fitting into the place where it belonged. Rogan. That frame-up, just now. Bull-neck and his playmates . . . the lookout and the bouncer . . . Mink Schwartz, staging a brawl that would wreck his place and lose him a steady customer . . . and now this girl, the girl Rogan wanted, according to Jim Hafey . . . Rogan, again. Maybe World Pete wanted that lease, now that a well had come in on it, more than Rogan wanted the girl . . . and if that fire kept on burning it wouldn't hurt World Pete's chances of getting what it wanted . . .

"Fifteen grand, waiting for us any time we want to grab it," Rick said, "and you get all steamed over a chance to go wild-catting!"

"Not wild-catting," Stella said. "Redheading."

"Skip it," Rick told her. He kept on looking at Dusty. "Listen, Duss. If you got to let a jane sink her hooks in you, pick the kind that tries to make you like it. Not the kind that figures you're a blanket Osage with gold spittoons in your wigwam. This redhead never turned a hair when I kept telling her she was asking us to take a chance on getting cooked, did she? Not her! Guys like you and me don't look human to her. She thinks she's doing us a favor just by living in the same world with us, and anything she can take us for is coming to her, and not even a tip coming back. You'd be safer fooling around her fire than around her."

"I'm not so sure," Stella said. "It looked to me as if she might go for Dusty. We're funny, us girls."

"You mean phoney," Rick snapped at her. "What's the idea? Duss don't need any help to make a sucker out of himself. Lay off."

"What's all the shooting for?" Dusty said. "She looked to me like a nice kid in a tough spot, that's all. We could let it go at that, couldn't we?"

Rick kept on looking sore for a second. Then he laughed.

"Sure. We let it go at that, and get back to business."

He swung around to the dice game. Over his shoulder Stella caught Dusty's eye and jerked her head towards the door. He knew she only wanted to get rid of him so she'd have Rick to herself, with nobody between her and what was left of the bankroll, but as he turned away he caught himself feeling almost friendly toward her.

He stopped when he got to the door that led into the front room. Dan Rogan, still looking as if his linen suit had been frosted on him like the icing on a cake, stood at one end of the long chromium bar. He had got his smile out of the ice-box again and he was using it on Jan Morel. More than ever, under the black brows, his eyes looked like two dimes. Dusty had never felt that way before, but all at once he seemed to know exactly how a dog feels when it growls.

He went over toward them. Rogan only nodded at him but when Jan looked around and saw him there was something in her face that, without knowing it, Dusty must have been hoping would be there. It made him feel as if he'd found something that he'd thought was lost. Then it was gone, and Jan stood up a little straighter, and turned, slowly, back to Rogan.

"That's awfully kind of you, Mr. Rogan. I——"

"Make it Dan," Rogan said. The growl was almost real inside of Dusty. It didn't make him feel any better when Jan laughed.

"All right, Dan, then."

She said it lightly. There wasn't any real friendliness behind it. Even Dusty could tell that. He felt better.

She gave Rogan a nod and started for the door. She gave Dusty a smaller nod, going by him. He didn't blame her for that. She had a right to be sore at him, after what she'd taken from Rick. He went out after her.

Rogan's eyes followed him to the doorway; the smile was gone and the black eyebrows were pulled a little nearer together, and the white, careful fingers, rubbing out a half-smoked cigarette, bore down a little more heavily than was needful. More than ever, as Rogan went into the back room, his mouth looked like a buttonhole.

He put the smile back on again, though, for Stella Conway. Rick had moved over to the chuck-a-luck game, and Stella, playing with silver dollars, was thriftily coppering Rick's twenty-dollar bets, and luck, using the word as gamblers like Mink Schwartz understood it, was dealing very kindly with her. It wasn't necessary for Rogan to ask Stella to call him Dan. She did it in a voice that jerked Rick around from the table, the dead-pan look in his face.

"If it's business, skip it, Rogan. You'll have Mink charging me office-rent, the first thing you know."

"You might be glad to pay it," Rogan said. "How would twenty—" he hesitated only for a split second but it was long enough to consider the next figure that had been in his mind and give himself the pleasure of cutting it in half—"how would twenty-two five sound to you, for the Bayou Rouge job?"

Rick looked at Stella. "Did you hear what I heard? Twenty-two five! And every nickel of it hurting this guy like losing four front teeth!"

"Why would it?" Stella said. "It's World Pete money."

"That wouldn't make him like it," Rick said. "It's an icepick through his big heart to watch anybody except him getting that kind of dough, no matter who it's coming out of."

Rogan's expression didn't change.

"How about it?" he said.

"Take your foot out of the door," Rick said. "We don't want any."

"Twenty-five," Rogan said.

Rick looked him over.

"That fire must be burning a hole right through your guts!"

"Take it or leave it." The edge of Rogan's voice was just a little ragged. "This is the roof."

"Take it, Rick." Stella spoke in a quick whisper.

"Don't worry, kid. I'm taking it. Hey, Duss——" he ran a swift look around the room, and crooked a finger at a waiter. "Go out in the bar and tell Duss Miller to come in here."

"He might have to go a little further than the bar," Rogan said. "My guess would be about ten miles out on the Saragossa road."

Rick's head jerked up.

"Saragossa!"

"It's only a guess," Rogan said. "But that's where Miss Morel was going, and judging by the look on Miller's face when he went out after her, I wouldn't be surprised if he'd gone along."

Rick kicked a stool over behind him in his hurry to get to the door. Stella moved a little closer to Rogan.

"You work fast, don't you, Dan?"

"I try to," Rogan said. He studied her, taking his time about it. "Any special reason for the remark?"

"Oh, not exactly special," Stella said. "I just noticed that after that first play went wrong it hardly took you any time at all to get here with another one."

"What play?" Rogan's voice was very quiet.

"Why, you know. The little surprise party you had Mink Schwartz arrange for Rick and Dusty just now. The one that was going to put them in a nice quiet hospital, where they wouldn't have to fight any fires for a long, long time."

"I thought you didn't drink," Rogan said.

"And when that didn't work you were right here with one that did work," Stella went on, as if she hadn't heard him. "I do hope the higher-ups at World Pete know how much trouble you've taken to make sure that Saragossa fire doesn't get put out too soon."

"When am I supposed to laugh?" Rogan said.

"Oh, the funny part hasn't come yet." Stella moved the emerald so that the light struck green fire from it. "The funny part was my happening to be talking to Jim Hafey, a while ago, just when somebody called him on the telephone. He didn't shut the door of the booth, at first, and you know how he always shouts, especially when he's had a few drinks. Of course, I couldn't hear what you were saying, but——"

She stopped and began playing with the ring again.

"It's a pity," Rogan said. "Smart enough to guess so many answers and not smart enough to keep them to yourself."

"Oh, I'm smart enough to do that, too." Stella slid a hand through the bend of a starched sleeve. "I've kept them to myself so far and I'm almost sure I could keep on doing it if—if somebody took a little trouble to talk me into it."

The two dimes looked her over.

"Don't worry," Rogan said. "Somebody will."

5

JAN MOREL was just opening the door of the old Pierce Arrow when Dusty caught up with her. She turned, holding herself stiffly straight.

"Well?" Her voice was straight, too, and stiff.

"I wanted to talk to you a minute," Dusty said.

She hesitated. "All right. But it'll have to be on the way. I can't spare any more time. Get in."

Dusty followed her into the car. The seat was so high off the ground that it felt like riding on top of a bus. The gears clashed and chattered, and he could feel the throb of the old motor, but he got a queer sense of power and strength. Being old, he thought, was one sign of being tough. The street, bright with flood-lighting, made him think again of two towns trying to grow in the same place. The old Beauport was still here, in between the skyscrapers and the neon signs and the hotspots, and acting, somehow, as if it didn't know they were there. The Pierce Arrow was part of that older town and time, and so was Jan Morel, for all her young aliveness.

"I was kind of sorry about all that," Dusty said.

"I could see you were," Jan said.

"You got Rick all wrong. He isn't that way, inside. It's only when we've just got through a job. You hit it pretty close when you made that crack about us being sailors on a spree, only it wasn't liquor that keyed Rick up, but being half an eyelash away from getting rubbed out. That's the only time he's all the way alive, and it always gets him high. It's pretty much the same as if he'd been on a bender, and then, just when he's starting to taper down, you try to start him in all over again, see? He couldn't stand even hearing about it."

"Never mind about him," Jan said. "You can

stand hearing about it or you wouldn't be here. That's really why you came after me, isn't it?"

"It won't do any good," Dusty said. "Rick's turned the proposition down and that settles it. But I did sort of want to know what we're passing up."

"You're passing a pretty good thing," she said. "I'd made up my mind to go as high as a tenth interest in the lease if I had to, and once the fire's out that's worth more than any cash price you'd have charged me. Maybe fifty times as much, or a hundred. If we had money or time I wouldn't be offering it, but we haven't."

She hesitated. Dusty didn't say anything.

"I'm putting the cards on the table. We've put just about every cent we had or could borrow into this lease. I have to raise money and raise it in a hurry and I won't stand much chance of doing it till the fire's out. I've got to get somebody to put it out and all I have to offer is an interest in the lease. It's incorporated. The M-H Oil Company. A hundred thousand shares. Dad and Jim Hafey each own forty-five thousand and——"

"How did Hafey get that much?" Dusty said.

"We had to give it to him before he'd come in with us on one more well. We'd already drilled three dry holes and nobody but a plunger like Jim would have come in at all. Even he wouldn't have, if he hadn't been so hard up that he couldn't move his rig. He gets his stock just for letting us use the rig and for overseeing the job and I hope he makes a billion out of it."

"That wouldn't stop Jim Hafey from dying broke," Dusty said. "Go ahead. He's got forty-five per cent."

"He owns it, but he hasn't got it. He's put it up as collateral on his loans. Dad's done that with his, too. But I own the odd ten thousand shares and I've got them. I was going to offer you and your partner part of them, or even all of them, if I had to. I know it isn't good business to tell you so, but I'm putting the cards on the table, just as I said. Dad and Jim would say I'm crazy to offer that much, but Dad's up in St. Louis in a hospital and Jim's off on one of his sprees, drowning his worries, and I have to use my own judgment. Ten per cent of that lease may be a lot too much to pay for putting out a fire, but I can't help it and I don't care. With the fire out Dad's share will be worth enough for both of us. More than enough. Even a tenth interest will be worth——"

"Plenty, maybe, and then again maybe not," Dusty said. "No telling how much oil is down there. Even with the fire out, it's still a blind gamble from our end."

"Yes. But a gamble that's worth taking! Not Rick Farren's kind." There was a sudden heat in her voice. "Not gambling just for the silly fun of it, just for the chance of keeping on if you win, but gambling for the chance of never having to do it again! The kind I've been doing, stretching out half a shoestring long enough to reach down to oil. I've had fun doing it. Even the worry's been fun, in a way. But it was fun because what I was playing for was my chance of never having to do it again."

"I know," Dusty said. "I've felt like that myself, once in a while. It sounded good to me, tonight, when you were trying to make Rick see it."

"I knew it did. That's why I kept on trying. I could see you were different from your—your partner!" She said the word as if it was something she'd picked up gingerly, with tips of her fingers, and was holding away from her.

"Don't get Rick wrong," Dusty said. "Rick's aces, every way. Take it from me. In our business if there's a soft spot in the man you're working with you find it out on your first job. If it wasn't for Rick, I'd be——"

"You'd be putting out this fire for me," Jan said.

"Me?" Dusty had to laugh, in spite of not feeling like it.

"Yes, you. The minute I saw the two of you tonight I knew which one of you I had to get. I knew you could do this job, whether Rick Farren helped or not." She stopped. "Will you do it? There'll be plenty of men out there to help you. Good ones. Guthead Marr and Ivan Gary and——"

"Listen," Dusty said. "Any time Rick and I split up it won't be me that does it. It's no use talking about my walking out on him. When he picked me out of the mud I was nothing but an oil bum. I couldn't even hold down a roustabout's job. I came out to this country the same way kids used to run away to punch cows and fight Indians. Only when they got out west what they were looking for wasn't there any more, and what I was looking for was right here. All of it. Everything was just the way I'd hoped it would be. Everything but me. I didn't fit into the picture. I didn't have what it takes."

"How do you mean?" Jan said.

"I guess you have to be born in the oil country and grow up in it, like Rick, to be a real oil man," he said. "Back where I came from everything was settled and safe and the only way anybody ever tried to change anything was to make it safer and softer. Before you can talk you're getting it rubbed into you that it's a sin to take a chance unless you have to. I'm not trying to alibi myself. I'm just trying to make you see why I wasn't any use out here till I got teamed with Rick and why I wouldn't be any use without him."

"I think you would," she said. "I think you——"

"That's because you don't know. But it doesn't matter. Because I'd be sticking with Rick anyway. He was tops in the business when he took me on, and I was nothing, net. He took a chance on me when nobody else would have done it, and when it meant a lot to him if he was guessing wrong. He's been taking that same chance on every job we've tackled for almost six years. You wouldn't know how I feel about it, but——"

"Yes. I think I do know, now." Her voice was different. "I think I'd feel the same way in your place. But you could come out with me, couldn't you, and look the fire over. You wouldn't be going back on him if you told us how to put it out, would you?"

"That's what I was going to put up to you," Dusty said. "I kind of wanted to help, any way I could. I hated to see a—to see you in a jam like this and not do anything about it. Specially after I saw Dan Rogan with you."

"Dan Rogan? What's he got to do with it?"

"Nothing, maybe. Only he works for World Pete, and this fire isn't hurting World Pete's chance of edging in on your jackpot. And just about the time when the news that your well was on fire would be hitting town, a bunch of strongarms drifted into Mink Schwartz's place and made a nice try at wishing a brawl on Rick and me. You came in just in time to see the finish of it. It's been quite a while since anybody wanted trouble bad enough to pick on Rick and me just for the hell of it. So it looked as if maybe somebody was figuring we might go after your fire for you and was trying to make sure we wouldn't be in shape to do it. And when I heard Rogan asking you to call him Dan——"

"You sound like Jim Hafey! Just because Dan Rogan's with World Pete he must be back of any dirty work that's doing and plenty that isn't! He went out of his way to be decent to me, tonight. He stopped me just to send word to Jim that he'll help any way he can, and all that'll mean to Jim is that World Pete is getting ready to knife us in the back!"

"If it was my back I'd be looking over my shoulder," Dusty said.

"Oh——" She sounded angry, but if she was she changed her mind abruptly about showing it. "All right. I'll be looking over mine, then. Here we are."

They were out beyond the edge of the town. She turned into a driveway between liveoaks and magnolias. The headlights brought white pillars and a long gallery out of the night, for a moment, and, moving on, let them go back into it. The car stopped. Jan slid out.

"I'll only be a minute. Just long enough to get into levis."

"Okay," Dusty said. He could see she'd rather not ask him inside to wait. He didn't blame her for that. He was part of the new Beauport. He didn't belong in there, in the old one. She could go back and forth across that line, but he couldn't. Seeing that, knowing it was true, made him wish it wasn't true. But it was. With the headlights out the house was only a dim whiteness, but he could feel it looking down at him. It wasn't unfriendly; it just didn't know him, that was all. Or want to know him.

It was longer, by a good deal, than a minute, before Jan came running down the wide steps.

"I'm sorry but I wanted to find out about Dad and the St. Louis wire was busy."

"How's he making out?" Dusty said.

"He's having a pretty bad time of it, but they say he'll be all right. I hope he doesn't hear about the fire. I told them not to tell him anything except that the well was in."

She slid in behind the wheel. The dash-lamp showed Dusty that she had on overalls and high laced boots, a checked shirt and a round felt hat. He felt as if she had changed into somebody different from the tall girl in the misty green dress, as if that girl had stayed beyond, in the house where she belonged. This one, sending the old Pierce roaring along the concrete, was alive and real and awake; she fitted into the world he lived in, was herself a part of it. He ought to like her better than the other one; he did like her better. But he kept on liking the other one, too, and being sorry she had stayed behind.

Sixty was about all the Pierce would do. It was quite a while before they could see the yellow brightness, spreading up from the skyline ahead.

"I guess I've been hoping the boys had managed to put it out." Jan laughed a little. "It seems to hit me harder, finding they haven't, than I thought it would."

"Funny. That's just what I was thinking," Dusty said. It was only half true. Nobody hated a fire the way he did, but if this one had been licked it would have meant that there wouldn't be anything, any more, to be a sort of bridge between him and Jan Morel. "Don't let it get you down, though. You didn't have anything out there to fight a fire with, and most of 'em take plenty. Just because it's still going strong doesn't mean you aren't going to lick it."

"I know. I wouldn't be worried if——" she stopped. "Don't misunderstand this, will you? I'm not trying to talk you out of sticking with Rick. I know you've got to and I'd—I guess I'd think you were a heel if you didn't. But suppose he was willing to take on the job, how would you feel about it?"

"That's an easy one. Anything Rick says is all right with me. But——"

"I didn't mean that, exactly. I meant—suppose it was up to you? Suppose he left it to you?"

"He won't," Dusty said.

"I know. But suppose he did. Would you take it on?"

"In a minute," Dusty said. "I liked your proposition, right from the start. I told Rick so. But he doesn't like it, and he never will, and that's that.

It's no use talking about what I'd do if I was calling signals. I don't call 'em, and I won't be calling 'em."

"No. It's no use, but all the same I'm glad to know you see it my way. I thought you did, but I wanted to be sure. I hate being wrong about people, I mean, and I wanted to be right about you. About our—our being on the same side of the fence. That's what I thought, back there at the Winter Garden. I kept feeling as if you didn't belong there, any more than I did. And you don't, either."

"Well," Dusty said, "I don't get much of a kick out of watching the dice roll, if that's what you mean."

"It's part of it." She didn't go on. The brightness ahead was brighter now, and higher up from the skyline. The Pierce pounded toward it, like an old fire-horse that smelled smoke. They turned off the concrete and bumped over potholes hidden under the deep red dust of a dirt road. Ahead, above the scrub woods the sky itself was fire, the tree-tops black against it, and even above the noises of the car Dusty could hear the fire—the sound of it beat against his ears, the way that sound always did, like the snarl of a beast, furious, blood-thirsting. He set his teeth against it.

Where the plank road crossed the swampy stretch, flashes of hard light shot up from the black puddles. There was a string of other cars ahead, suddenly distinct against the fire. And the nearest of them was one that Dusty knew. The sight of it pulled a shout out of him.

"I told you Rick was aces! There's our car! He's here!"

Ahead, against the glare, a little crowd of people looked like black cutouts on orange paper. Two of them came walking back toward the cars. One of them was Rick, with big Jim Hafey a step behind him. Something about Rick's face worried Dusty a little.

"Well, look who's here!" Rick had a trick of talking, without seeming to lift his voice, so that you could hear him through the uproar of a fire. "Hiya, sister. Who's your Indian friend?"

"I'm sorry about that." Jan had to scream, but even screaming didn't thin down her voice and sharpen it, like most women's voices when they were loud.

"Don't be," Rick said. "It's a swell crack. You got us right. That's what we are—just a couple of Osages, blowing ourselves to gold spittoons."

"I'm sorry," Jan said again. "I just saw red, for a minute. I thought you meant it when you turned me down, and——"

"Yeah. And now you think I didn't mean it, I got nice white wings, huh?" Rick laughed. "Don't kid yourself, Toots. I meant it, all right."

Dusty could almost feel it hit her. But she took it smiling.

"Oh. I thought——" she stopped. "Then why——?"

"Why am I here?" Rick laughed again. "You ought to guess that one. You didn't figure I'd let you get away with this play, did you?"

"What play?" Jan said.

"That's right. Act dumb. You only brought Duss out to get the fresh air. You never even thought about glamoring the poor sucker into walking out on me and taking a crack at your fire on his own. Sure you didn't. You just——"

"Take it easy, Rick." Dusty pushed in between

them. "You ought to know how much chance there is of my rawdealing you. I came out to take a look, that's all. Any complaints?"

Rick looked him over, his eyes half shut, his face deadpan. Then he shook his head.

"No complaints, kid. Go get your look. Take it from me, that'll be all you'll want of this baby."

Dusty had already seen enough to know that this was close to the truth. He went ahead a few steps, though, the crowd splitting to give him passage-room. Without dark glasses he couldn't look at the brightness for more than a split second at a time, but that was long enough. The burning gas came shooting almost flat in a sort of giant toadstool, maybe a hundred feet across. In that circle and for maybe another hundred feet all around it, everything that could burn was gone. The mud was baked to brick, the trees that were left standing at the outer rim showed red embers on their fireward side. Dusty picked a path around the edge of the heat. He didn't see much chance that anything alive would ever get in close enough to put a hook into the wreckage.

He came back to where Jan and Rick and Jim

Hafey were waiting. Jan's eyes, more green than gray in the poison brightness, were asking him the questions he didn't want to answer.

"No use trying to talk this close," he shouted to her. They all went back to the car. Even here it took that trick voice of Rick's to make itself heard without yelling.

"I hear you're going to tell us how to lick it. Okay, Fire Chief. Shoot."

All Dusty could do was to shake his head. He hated to watch the hopefulness going out of Jan's face, but there wasn't any way to keep it there. Jim Hafey moved over beside her and bent a big arm around her. Dusty liked him for that. Hafey had the name of being a good loser and he was living up to it. Under the soot and sweat and tiredness his plump face was almost cheerful.

"What? No bright ideas?" Rick said. "Well, come on, then. We got a job waiting for us, down at Bayou Rouge."

Dusty stared at him.

"Yeah," Rick said. "You were in such a sweat to get back to business I didn't have the heart to keep you waiting. And Rogan's paying us twenty-five thousand, ready-to-spend money. Not wallpaper."

Dusty didn't want to look at Jan but he couldn't seem to help it. He could see what she was thinking.

"What did I tell you about Dan Rogan, Jan?" Hafey was still being the good loser. He sounded as if it was just a laugh. "Any time he sees a friend of his in a jam, that big heart of his comes right up in his throat and chokes him! He can't bear to see you and me drown so he tosses us an anvil! All the reason he's bidding the boys up so high is to make dead sure this fire burns us down to where World Pete can grab us without even stretching."

The stubborn look came into Jan's face.

"That isn't fair, Jim. Why should Dan Rogan let a World Pete fire go on burning just to do us a favor? And—" her eyes went by Dusty's without stopping, as if they didn't see him—"and nobody needs to hire Mr. Farren—" again it seemed to Dusty that she picked up the name in the tips of her fingers and held it away from her—"to let this fire of ours alone. You'd do that for nothing, wouldn't you, Mr. Farren?"

"I was waiting for you to pull that one," Rick said. "If we won't wade in there after a piece of conversation money, maybe we'll do it on a dare. It's a good play. It's got whiskers on it, but it's still good. Only not good enough, see? Try another."

Jan shook her head.

"No. I can see you're too clever for me, Mr. Farren." She turned to Dusty, holding out her hand. "Thanks for coming out. Good luck on the other job."

Her hand was hard, and it gave him a quick, strong grip, like a man's. He could see she wasn't blaming him for standing by Rick, the way some women would have. She knew he had to.

"I'm sorry," he said.

"I know you are." She gave him a quick smile. "Good-night."

She turned and started back towards the fire. Jim Hafey stayed behind. His face looked like a pink egg.

"I let you get by with it this once, Farren, because I could see it was the first time you ever talked to any kind of a woman but the cheap tramps you go for, and I got my hands plenty full, right now, without taking out time to give you what's coming to you. But it'll be waiting for you, any time you come back after it. Get going, keep going and stay gone, see?"

Dusty liked the fat old fellow better than ever. The crowd had moved back to them and pushed in close enough to hear, and half a dozen of Hafey's crew were in it, Guthead Marr and Ivan Gary and Odd Shape Pender, so there'd be plenty to mix in if anything started, but Hafey's back was toward them and as far as he knew he was playing the hand alone. Dusty's hat was off to him. And so, it turned out, was Rick's.

"Okay, Jim. I asked for it and I'm taking it. Come on, Duss."

Dusty didn't need to be urged. He was in the car ahead of Rick. Rick snaked it out of line and backed it, fast, shaving the edge of the road, till there was room to turn. He didn't say anything till they were on the concrete, doing eighty. Talking was never any fun for Rick when he was driving slowly enough to make it safe.

"Sorry, Duss. I ought to have known you wouldn't

two-time me. But I could see the redhead was under your skin, and when Rogan said you'd started out here with her——"

"Rogan, eh?" The name suddenly gave Dusty the beginnings of an idea. Nobody could ever change Rick's mind for him, once he'd made it up, but he might change it for himself if he was handled right. And Dusty could see a way to handle him. He thought for a few moments before he made his first move. "So it was Rogan that sold you the idea I was running out on you, was it?"

"I said I ought to've known better, didn't I?" Rick's voice sharpened a little. That was the way Dusty wanted it to sound.

"It's all right with me, Rick. I don't blame you for falling for it. Rogan's good. And giving you the notion that I was double-crossing you would be easy for him, compared to the rest of what he's putting over on us."

"What do you mean, putting over on us?" The voice was ugly, now. Almost as ugly as Dusty wanted it to be.

"He's got us going after his Bayou Rouge fire,

hasn't he, after we've been turning him down cold on it? That would be a score for him, no matter how much he pays us, even if it was all he was getting. And he's getting plenty besides. Hafey called it right. Rogan wants that Morel lease and he wants it a whole lot. He wants it enough to hang up ten thousand extra just to make it a little surer that we don't stay up here and douse this fire. If he can keep it burning the lease drops in his lap, and what he pays us for the Bayou Rouge job comes back into his pocket with plenty more on top of it. Instead of its costing him money to get his fire licked, we hand him a sweet profit on it."

"So what?" Rick said. "So Rogan's using his head. Would that be news? All that interests me is that he's laying bigger money on the line than we ever took down on any other job."

"Yes," Dusty said. He could see his way clearly, now. "That's what interests me, too. I keep wondering how much more he might lay on that line if we played him right. The twenty-five grand was his figure, wasn't it?"

"So what?" Rick said again. But he said it differently this time.

"Nothing. Only if he went to his top price of his own accord it's a new record. It'd be more like him to start at the bottom and work up. And no farther up than he had to."

Rick didn't say anything, but the car put another five miles or so on top of the eighty. For once Dusty didn't mind that.

"If my guess is right and we've got a chance to sink the harpoon in that baby I'd kind of like to sink it nice and deep. I'd sort of like to charge him something extra for handing you the idea I was crossing you."

Still Rick didn't answer. Dusty gave him a little while to think.

"And I wouldn't mind leveling with him for the fast one he tried to pull on us at Mink Schwartz's, either."

"What fast one?" Rick said. Dusty had been hoping he hadn't got around, yet, to figuring out that frame-up.

"Those playboys that wanted to wrestle," he said. "You don't think that just happened, do you? Since when did anybody want trouble bad enough to ask you and me for it? Those gorillas were there on business. One of 'em was just shaking a sap down out of his cuff when Stella cracked that glass. Maybe it's just my evil mind but I can't help wondering whether good old Danny Rogan wasn't trying out a cheap way of keeping you and me away from this fire before he fell back on a play that would cost him real money."

He waited again. Rick didn't talk, but the way he was driving talked for him.

"Of course twenty-five thousand is heavy sugar, for guys like you and me," Dusty said. "We ought to be tickled to death at the chance to grab it, even if we earn Dan Rogan a dollar for every dime we make for ourselves. But——"

"Skip the double-talk," Rick said. "I'm a long way ahead of you. Right now I'm working on what I'm going to say when I get to a phone and wake that wise guy up to hear what he can do with his twenty-five grand and his fire and——"

"And see if he cares," Dusty said. "His fire's been going strong for a couple of weeks and he's still taking nourishment. He wouldn't mind getting it doused, of course, but what he really wants is this Morel lease. My idea of really spoiling his night's sleep would be to slip him the news that we're passing up his job so as to tackle this one."

"I was ahead of you on that, too," Rick said. "I been watching you working around to the real play. Get me sore enough at Rogan and maybe I'll go lick the redhead's fire so as to spite him. And the redhead pastes a gold star on your report-card and we split up a piece of bright blue sky and Rogan bites himself in the arm and dies of it. It's a swell idea, but there's a hole in it. This is one fire that's got us stopped before we start, and if the redhead didn't have you slap-dizzy you'd know it."

"I do know it," Dusty said. "I don't see how we even start after this one. But there's no law against our putting up a bluff at going after it, is there? A good enough bluff to give Rogan the idea we mean business?"

Maybe that was all it would amount to. Maybe, even if he succeeded in talking Rick into giving him the chance to look for a way to beat this fire, he wouldn't be able to find one. But he might find one.

He'd found ways, before now, of licking a few pretty bad ones.

"Go on from there," Rick said. He didn't quite manage to keep from sounding interested. That was all Dusty wanted.

"Well, while we're sticking around making a few passes at it, what does Rogan do? If my hunch is right and he wants that lease as badly as I figure he does, he'll be sweating blood, won't he?"

Rick laughed.

"Not blood," he said. "Rogan don't use it. He sweats ice-water and bleeds pennies."

Dusty gave him the chuckle he knew he wanted.

"And they both hurt him plenty," he said. "I'm betting he drops around every little while and boosts his price on the Bayou Rouge job. And if he doesn't, what have we got to lose? Nobody else is going to lick that one for him. It'll be right there, waiting for us, any time we want to go after it."

The car slowed down a little.

"You got something there," Rick said. "We'll play it your way. Only don't get the idea you're putting anything over. I know what's on your mind, all right.

You're kidding yourself that there might be a way for us to douse the redhead's fire for her and live happy ever after on the piece of the lease."

"Sure I am." Dusty knew better than to try any covering up. "It's one chance in a million, maybe, but we're playing it free, aren't we? And win or lose we'll be jacking up our price on the Bayou Rouge job, on top of sinking a few hooks in Rogan."

"Yeah," Rick said. "And on top of that we might be handing you a swell build-up with the redhead, huh?"

"Oh, be your age," Dusty said. "She just happens to be mixed up in what looks to me like our chance for a real score, that's all. You said yourself that guys like us don't look human to her. I'm not dumb enough to kid myself into——"

"You won't need to kid yourself," Rick said. "That'll be handled for you, as long as that jill figures it's worth her while. So watch your step, if you want to go through with this play." He held up his right hand with the first two fingers crossed. "King's X on the redhead, see? The first time I spot you even looking thirsty at her, all bets are off."

"All right." It was no trouble for Dusty to sign off that way. He was looking ahead, thinking how Jan's face would light when he told her. If the world had been twice as high he'd still have been on top of it.

6

THE PIERCE ARROW was in the driveway under the magnolias, so that Dusty could stop wondering whether Jan had got back from the well. By daylight the pillars and galleries weren't white, but gray, with the paint peeling off them, and there was a sag in the wide steps, but these things only made the house look friendlier to Dusty, or not friendly, exactly, either, but more as if it was trying to remember where it had seen him before.

Rick made a crack about Gone With The Wind but Dusty hardly heard him. He got a kick out of just going up the steps. Instead of a button beside the door there was a silver knob, and when Rick pulled it a bell tinkled, instead of buzzing, a quiet, gentle sound a long way off. After quite a while the door opened a little way. A colored woman, bulging out inside of a white apron like a rolled mattress tied in the middle, looked out through the gap. Her eye showed yellow like a mustang's.

"We want to see Miss Morel," Dusty said.

The mustang eye rolled his way.

"No suh. I ain't go' wake her up for nobody."

The door started closing. Rick got his foot in its way. That turned out to be a mistake, though; the door kept right on closing. Rick pounded on it with the heel of his hand. "Hey. Go easy."

"What is it, Zenie?" Jan's voice, from somewhere overhead, reminded Dusty of the sound of the old doorbell. It was the kind of a voice, for all the tiredness in it, that belonged in a house like this.

"It's me, Jan. Duss Miller. Rick and I want to talk to you."

"All right. I'll be down in a minute." The voice changed. "Stop your nonsense, Zenie. Let the gentlemen in."

The door swung inward with Zenie making clucking sounds behind it like an angry hen. The hall was cool and almost dark. It was almost empty, too, with only a funny looking old sofa against one side wall and a wide, spidery-railed stairway making a lazy climb up along the other one. It was the first time Dusty had ever seen the inside of one of these old-timers but he seemed to have known that it would be like this. It was a million miles from the New England hallways he remembered and yet there was something in its emptiness that he had always found in them; it was in the long, dim room where Zenie left them, too. He felt at home here, as if he had always lived in rooms with bare floors of wide, time-colored oaken boards, rooms where the serenely shabby chairs seemed to have placed themselves at comfortable random instead of standing at attention like stiff-backed soldiers on parade.

Rick clowned a shiver.

"The Old Plantation, just like back before the war! I'll take the morgue."

Even that was right, somehow, Dusty thought. That was the way Rick ought to feel about it. He'd feel the same way about those white-panelled rooms back in Vermont that Dusty was remembering. They weren't much like the shacks and mud of the oil-boom towns where Rick had grown up, and still less like the brassy swank of the shiny new hotels he lived in now and the chromium nightspots where he found his fun. All at once, Dusty caught himself feeling a little sorry for Rick, and it startled him, because he'd never felt that way before.

"Listen," Rick said. "You're getting your way about taking on this job, but the business end of it is going to be handled my way. When Red comes down I do the talking, see?"

"What's new about that?" Dusty said.

"I just want to make sure you keep out of it. Maybe you're only out to spike Rogan and maybe you're more interested in handing yourself a build-up with this redhead. I wouldn't know. But when she comes down she's doing business with me and not you. And she's doing it my way."

"How do you mean?" Dusty said.

"This is how. Maybe I don't know my women but I know this much. I know they're swell little collectors when they win and when they lose they want to pay off any way except in cash."

"Jan isn't that kind," Dusty began. "She——"

"In my book they're all that kind, and we're going by my book on this deal. Maybe, while we're making a bluff at licking this fire, we just happen to find a way to lick it, and if we do, we're collecting, see?"

"How do you mean?" Dusty said.

"I mean we're collecting. We take a chance on seeing a way to douse the fire and we take another on getting a few blisters, doing it. We take a chance on there being some oil left in that hole when and if we get the fire out. But there's one chance we don't take. We may be working for wallpaper but we get the wallpaper and we get it now. Any time I bet with a dame it doesn't go on the finger. It lays on the line."

"But I tell you——"

"I'm telling you," Rick said. "It's that way or else."

Dusty gave in.

"All right. It's that way then."

"Okay. That's one thing settled. And here's another. While we're tossing the harpoon into Rogan we'll just push it a little deeper. Hafey says he's carrying the torch for this redhead. If he is, and she asks him to lend us a little World Pete equipment to help us down her fire, how is Rogan going to smooth-talk himself out of it? Either he turns her down and looks like a louse to her or else he has to let us have whatever equipment we need, and look pleasant while we use it to keep World Pete from taking over her lease. Either way he bleeds, and see if I care!"

There wasn't time for Dusty to say anything. Heels clicked on the stairs and Jan came to the doorway. The short-skirted green dress made her look younger than she had seemed last night, but there were old shadows under her eyes and an old tiredness in the set of her lips.

"Well?" She sounded as if she didn't care much about finding out why they were here. Even when they looked at Dusty her eyes weren't interested; they were tired eyes, having a hard time staying open and they were looking at something that didn't matter to them, except that they'd rather have been looking at something else. Or at nothing.

"Sister, could you spare a smile?" Rick said. "Open, please. This isn't going to hurt a bit."

"Do you mind if I don't laugh?" Jan said. "I've been having quite a night and I'm afraid I'm not in the mood for——"

"Relax, Red. You'll be in the mood for this one. We changed our minds since we saw you. We're going to play Boy Scout and we got you picked out for our good deed. We're taking a crack at your fire."

Her head turned, quick as a bird's, toward Dusty. She didn't quite dare, yet, to start hoping, but her eyes were begging for the chance.

"That's right, Jan. Rick can't help clowning about it, but——"

"So I'm clowning," Rick said. "Okay. But don't get the idea I'm clowning about what comes next. You've won our hearts all right with your bright smile and your pretty ways, and we're coming over and play in your yard, but there's a string to it."

Some of the hopefulness went out of Jan's look, but she didn't say anything.

"You don't just promise us this piece of blue sky

we're working for," Rick went on. "You hand it to us in advance. If we can't lick your fire you get it back. Sure. Maybe we gyp you and hang onto it. That's the chance you're taking."

Jan laughed.

"Is that all? Of course you have the stock whenever you want it. I'll give it to you now. Wait a minute. I've got the certificate upstairs. I'll go get it for you."

She laughed again and went out. Her heels sounded happier, going up the stairs, than when they'd been coming down. The wind was out of Rick, for a second, but he got it back.

"How about it, kid? Do I handle 'em or do I handle 'em?"

"You're terrific," Dusty said. "You wasted it, though. Jan isn't the kind that would have——"

"How many more times do I have to tell you there's only one kind, and the label on the bottle says poison every time? If you're starting to kid yourself this dish is different, maybe we better go work for Rogan after all. One thing I gotta hand that guy—I don't have to fret about you wanting to play post-office with him."

Dusty knew he wanted a laugh on that one, and gave it to him. But he found his eyes looking over at the doorway, and all at once he was remembering another hallway, far away and long ago, where a gawky boy, all knees and elbows and redhot ears, had waited for a girl, all taffy hair and giggles, to give him his two registered letters and his parcel-post package. There could be worse games, at that, than postoffice.

Jan's heels clicked back down the stairs. She held a stock-certificate out to Rick.

"Here you are. It's endorsed in blank. Any time you fill in your name it's yours."

Rick looked it over.

"Ten thousand shares." He showed it to Dusty. "Look. We're big shots now—in the wallpaper business."

Jan laughed. Dusty could see he didn't have the top of the world to himself any more, but Jan's being up there too didn't seem to take any of the kick out of it for him.

"Where do we go from here?" she said.

"We stay right here." Rick folded the certificate

and put it in his pocket. "You're going to do a big favor for a friend of yours. You see we haven't said anything to Rogan yet. He's still feeling terrible over having to let his duty stop him from giving a little girl a hand. It'll be a big weight off his mind to hear we're working for you, and we figured you'd like to be the one to slip him the good news. So give him a buzz, will you? And while you're at it, you might kind of get his ideas about lending us a little World Pete equipment. We'd talk to him ourselves, only we don't know him the way you do, and you might have more luck. Of course there's other places to get what we need, but it'll take more time and cost more dough, and it won't be so good, either. World Pete's got the best there is and all of it."

Jan went to the telephone. She called a number and Rick angled a look at Dusty.

"I had a hunch this call wouldn't go through the switchboard. And Rogan's loose as ashes about giving out that private number."

Jan put her hand over the transmitter.

"See here, Rick——"

"That's right," Rick said. "Call me Rick. Play

your cards right and you might even get to know my private number."

Dusty would have been sore if Jan had given him a chance, but she didn't. She took it as a joke.

"Go on. Have your bright laughter. But try not to take my mind off what I'm doing, will you?—Hello—Mr. Rogan? What? Oh, all right, Dan, then." She made a funny face at Rick. "No. But I've got a right to sound cheerful. Only I'm afraid it won't make you feel that way. You see, I've hired your two smoke-eaters away from you. . . ."

The receiver made a sort of squeaky yelp.

"He's bleeding," Rick said. "I can hear the pennies."

". . . Thanks. I knew you'd be swell about it. . . . What? No. I didn't have to. They're taking a piece of the lease. . . . Yes. A tenth. . . . I don't care—I only hope it's worth a million. . . . I know you do, Dan. And that reminds me. The boys wondered if you could lend us some equipment. Oh, swell, Dan! . . . I knew you would . . . Yes . . . Yes . . . I'll tell them . . . I don't know how I'm ever going to thank you, but. . . . All right, I'll save it till I see you, but it'll be earning interest. Good-bye."

She hung up and turned. Her face was bright with the special kind of pleasedness that women save up to use on their I-told-you-so's.

"There! If there's anything we want that World Pete hasn't got, they'll get it for us. He says to tell McGoorty what you need, and if it isn't here they'll bring it up from Bayou Rouge." She stopped. "Well. Any comments?"

"Yeah," Rick said. "My hat's off to you. I always had an idea there was something kind of special about a redhead but I never would have figured that even a redhead could slip the needle into Dan Rogan. You're through for the day, sister. Go hit the horse-feathers. That's your end of it right now, taking good care of what you've got. No telling how long Rogan'll stay under the ether and we're liable to need you any minute to slip him another whiff."

All at once Dusty knew he couldn't take any more.

"Put on a new record, Rick. This one's starting to scratch."

"Okay, Butch." Rick's voice showed that there

were no hard feelings. He gave Jan a piece of a grin, about half of one. "The hay for yours, baby, and plenty of it, see. It'll be tomorrow before we can show you any action out there. We'll see you get tipped off in time to be there. So long."

"So long," Jan said, "and thanks."

There wasn't anything special in the way she looked at Dusty; it was just a smile, and a tired one at that. But he took it with him all the way out to the car and he could still see it when they were back at the Beauregard-McGee.

Stella was in the lobby; it was a habit with her, Dusty thought, happening to be wherever she could do herself a little good. She'd be easier to look at about twelve hours from now, but she wasn't very hard to look at, even now, especially after she quit pretending to be sore at Rick and gave him the wide, slow smile she saved up to use on him.

"You wouldn't remember me, Mr. Farren, but I'm the little girl you took the powder on, last night. Does it come back to you, now?"

"Okay." Rick didn't quite manage not to look guilty. "So I took a powder on you. What do you want me to do when I get it fixed so you're all alone with a Christmas tree like Dan Rogan—stick around and cramp your style?"

Stella pretended to be surprised.

"Oh, so you did it on purpose? Oh, dear! I'm so sorry I didn't guess. I thought you'd just forgotten I was there, and I couldn't help feeling a little hurt, and so, when Dan was so nice to me, I——" she put the ends of her fingers over her mouth. "Oh! And I practically promised him I wouldn't tell!"

Dusty knew she was only kidding; he could see, though, that Rick wasn't so sure about it. It was a queer thing, how Stella could always get him a little worried when she put on this act.

"Don't take it too hard," Rick said. "Rogan's been around. He's found out by now that once in a while a dame might go back on a promise. Go on. Spill it."

"Well, you see, I just happened to ask him if those boys who wanted to frolic with you, last night, were friends of his, and it worried him so to think of your getting such an idea about him that I almost had to promise him I wouldn't mention it to you. Please don't ever let him find out that I told you, will you? After the lovely big order he gave me——"

Rick hardly laughed out loud, but he did it now, and Dusty couldn't help joining in.

"I don't see what there is to laugh at," Stella said. "Why shouldn't he try some of our Marigold Hand Lotion? It's just as important for a man to keep his hands looking nice as for a woman."

"How about the Sweet Buttermilk Skin Food?" Rick said. "He could use a lot of that without doing his pan any harm."

"Yes. That's why I thought he'd better have a dozen jars of it. And—" Stella kept count on the fingers of her left hand, pushing them down like cash-register keys—"and I'm sure he'll like the Wild Primrose Bath Salts, too, and the Apple Blossom soap and the——"

Rick flagged her with a lifted hand.

"I never happened to tell you my idea about dames, did I, Duss? Does it add up? A sharpshooter like Dan Rogan taking a going-over from two of 'em in one day!"

Dusty stopped laughing.

"Jan didn't——"

"See? You know it and you don't believe it!" Rick said. "You——"

"All right. So I don't believe it. And we haven't got a thing to do but stick around here swapping gags."

Dusty managed to sound more good-natured than he felt, but not much more. Rick's face went deadpan, but only for a second.

"You might have something there, at that, Butch," he said. "Okay. We go find McGoorty. Maybe he didn't drop dead when Rogan told him World Pete was going Boy-Scout-minded."

7

"WE'RE on a dead card," Rick said.

He was watching Dan Rogan's big car starting back for town. Dusty was watching it too and not feeling any too cheerful about Jan Morel's being in it, even though, just before it disappeared into the scrub, she turned and waggled a gay, friendly arm back at him and Rick.

"We figured Rogan all wrong," Rick said. "He doesn't give half a damn for this lease or a dozen like it. All he wants is the redhead and all we're doing is to hand him a swell chance to make time with her. And is he making it!"

"He ought to be," Dusty said. He did a pretty fair job of pretending that he didn't care. "He's certainly breaking his neck to help her out of this jam. I even feel almost friendly toward the guy myself, when I think what he's doing for us."

"Us?" Rick stared.

"Sure. Us. We wouldn't stand a Chinese chance of licking this one if World Pete wasn't back of us. And we're going to lick it. I didn't think so, at first, but I was wrong. I can see how to get in there and put a hook onto that wreckage. That's what's shooting the fire out flat. If we can snake out the crownblock and the rotary and——"

"If," Rick said.

"When," Dusty said. "I can see how to do it. Fish out some of that junk and shoot the fire up straight enough to let us in there with a can of soup and it's in the bag."

"Maybe," Rick said.

"All right. Maybe, then. But I'm betting on it. This one doesn't stop us, after all."

"Maybe," Rick said again. He let it go at that, though, and Dusty felt a little safer. He knew he wouldn't have to be afraid of Rick's quitting any job after they once started on it. The danger was that Rick might quit before they started. And the sooner they got away from here the less chance there was of that. Out of sight of the fire, with his hands on a steering-wheel and his face turned towards town Rick couldn't help mellowing up a little. And there was no reason for staying here. They couldn't do anything till the World Pete crew finished drilling the new water well and McGoorty got his equipment up from Bayou Rouge.

Dusty started for the car, a little faster than he usually walked.

"What's your hurry?" Rick said. "You wouldn't have a date with the redhead, would you?"

"No chance. She's stepping out with Rogan."

Dusty knew he'd better sound cheerful about it. He did his best. It was good enough to get a grin out of Rick.

"And you're not carrying the torch?" He slid in behind the wheel. "Maybe you've got more brains than I've been giving you credit for."

"Maybe I have, at that," Dusty said. Trying to

tell Rick that he was wrong about Jan wouldn't help to put that fire out. He slid down in the seat, leaning back, and started singing Guthead Marr's song about the driller and the sleepy roughneck.

"Wake up, boy! Git your haid off that rock!
I hate to tell you, but it's twelve o'clock."

Rick shot a quick sidewise look at him.

"What keyed you up this high, all of a sudden?"

"Why wouldn't I be keyed up?" Dusty said. "We're cutting ourself a piece of cake, with good old Dan Rogan furnishing the knife."

He went on with the song.

"I hate to wake you, but I got it to do.
I don't need you but the contractor do."

Rick shot another look at him.

"If you're putting on an act, it's good," he said.

Dusty laughed and went on singing.

"Well, Mr. Driller, if that be true
You're gonna have a heap of fun.

If you pull that pipe this stormy night,
You'll wind her on the drum."

Rick chimed in with a second-tenor and they barbershopped all the way to the concrete. Here Rick could drive fast enough to stay happy and too fast for Dusty to take a chance on talking his eye off the road. But even so it was dark long before they pulled into the parking-lot behind the Beauregard-McGee, and there'd been time enough for Dusty to do a lot of thinking.

A good deal of it had been about Stella Conway. On the way across the lobby he stopped at the house-telephone and called her room. Throwing a party, instead of letting Rick do it, asking Stella to it, instead of waiting for her to crash it, had looked like a sound idea. When he hung up and turned around Rick's face told him that it had been very sound indeed.

"The Iridium Room, huh?"

"When I throw a party it gets throwed," Dusty said.

He could see he was on the right track. He stayed

on it. They went up to their suite and changed into the new white dinner jackets. By the time they got up to the Iridium Room, on top of the new wing, Stella was there, leaning back in a red-leather and chromium pipe chair. She took her time about getting out of it. It struck Dusty that everything Stella did looked as if somebody else was doing it for her. Even getting up out of a chair she made it seem as if something was lifting her out of it.

For once the slow smile she gave Dusty didn't bend downwards at the corners. Again he almost liked her. That was queer, because he knew she was going to make trouble for him. She'd do everything she could to stop Rick from taking on this Saragossa job in earnest. She always did her best to keep him from going back to work as long as there was any money left for him to blow in on her, and there was still plenty left over from the Rio Seco payoff. Handling Rick wasn't going to be easy, at the best of it; Stella would make it just as much harder as she could.

And yet, following her into the big gaudy room, Dusty kept on being tempted to like her. He guessed that maybe it was because she gave him even more of the invisible-man feeling than he got out of being with Rick.

The people who stared as she went by their tables didn't see Dusty. They didn't even see Rick. In her dead-black dress, with all the other women wearing colors, she might as well have been walking under a pencil spotlight. Her hair looked almost white and she'd been clever about not putting too much color on her face.

She even got to the headwaiter. He skittered in front of her, up high on his toes like a he-ballet-dancer, and it was her fault, Dusty guessed, that they got a table next to the dancing-space, with a reservation card on it.

Dusty ordered three champagne cocktails. Stella looked up from the card to slant another smile at him. It was friendly, like the other one, but it made him a little uneasy, all the same. Something in it reminded him, ridiculously, of the Grimfield school-house and the way Miss Pottinger had smiled when somebody with a guilty conscience put an apple on her desk.

"Don't pinch me just yet," Stella laughed. "I want to keep on dreaming this one. I'm Cleopatra and even that old woman-hating Dusty Miller is throwing parties for me, with champagne and everything. I know I'm going to wake up any minute but it's lovely while it lasts."

"You're awake," Rick said. "It's Duss that's having the bright dreams. He's celebrating because we're going to slap the redhead's fire down for her and get so lousy rich off our piece of the lease that she'll give Rogan the air and——"

"It's no dream about slapping down the fire, anyway." Dusty said it to Stella. She was the one he had to sell. With Rick on the fence it wouldn't be any trick at all for her to bring him down on the wrong side of it.

She kept on smiling but he couldn't tell what that meant. The headwaiter took their dinner order and skittered away with it, walking on soap bubbles. The cocktails came. Stella lifted hers and made a little flourish with it towards Dusty. She might be having fun with him before she spoiled his play or she might be going to help. He gave her back the gesture and the grin, and as soon as she'd finished her drink he stood up.

"Come on, dance with me this once, will you?"

She made believe to pinch her arm.

"Why, I'm awake! You really said it!"

"Come on," Dusty said again. Stella flashed a look at Rick. His face didn't tell Dusty anything about what he was thinking, but Stella must have found some meaning in it, because she let invisible hands lift her up, gently, to her feet. Dusty was a dub dancer, but two or three steps were all Stella needed to make him feel like a good one.

"Well, here we are. Alone at last." She laughed under her breath. Dusty didn't quite like the way it sounded. "Go on. What's on your mind that you didn't dare tell me in front of Rick?"

"This job," Dusty said. "I want to see it through. Rick doesn't, but I might be able to talk him into it, if you'll help instead of hindering."

She didn't say anything. He could guess what she was waiting for. It just wouldn't occur to Stella that anybody would ask a favor of her and let it go at that. The way she looked at things he wouldn't really have said anything till he'd told her what there'd be in it for her if she played ball with him.

"This might be your big chance," he said. "And it doesn't cost you a dime to play it."

She pulled away from him a little, far enough to get a quick look at his face. There was something in hers that he'd never seen there before. A new kind of hardness.

"Diagram that one for me." Her voice had the same kind of hardness.

"We can lick this fire. If we do, it might move Rick up into the real money and keep him there."

"So what?"

"Don't be like that," Dusty said impatiently. "You've never bothered to throw any bluffs. It's one thing I've always liked about you. I——"

"One?" She pretended to be surprised. "I never guessed there were that many."

"Look," Dusty said. "Let's skip the cross-talk. You're too good for me at it, and it doesn't get us anywhere. We both know you've got time for Rick when he's in the money and if not, not. The way things are he's in it every now and then, for a little while, and in between times you're back in the paint and powder business. All right. Here's a job that might put him on the plush for life. If it doesn't pay off you're right where you are now and if it does he won't ever need to fool around another fire and you won't ever need to peddle another lipstick. So how do you vote?"

"There's a question!" She laughed, and again Dusty seemed to notice something different in the cool hardness of the sound. "Knowing all you know about me, you have to ask me whether I'm passing up this kind of a chance to do myself some good!"

It was what he'd wanted her to say, but he didn't quite like the way she'd said it.

"I didn't think you'd get sore at me for playing the cards face up. You always play yours that way."

"I'm not sore." This time her laugh wasn't so hard. For once there was something in it that was almost friendly. "Let's stop talking and just dance."

That suited Dusty. Talking had been keeping his mind off the fun of dancing with somebody who had somehow cured him of having two left feet. He got along even better, though, when Stella started singing, under her breath, the song the band was playing.

"Here I go, down to the foot of the class again.
The same old examination, and I'll fail to pass again . . ."

Her voice was low-pitched and huskily sweet. If he hadn't known better he might almost have believed there was real feeling underneath it.

"Here I go, making the same dumb guesses—
Instead of noes, I'll put down yeses . . ."

It didn't make sense, knowing her for what she was, to let that small, whispery voice fool him into being sorry for her, into feeling as if she was singing those words about herself, as if there was truth in them, and yet——

"Oh, yes. I know all the answers, but I'm sunk again
Before I even start.
Oh, yes. I know all the answers, but I'm going to flunk again—
I only know them—by heart!"

The music stopped just as they were back near the table. Rick got up, his deadpan look a little deader than usual, and pulled back Stella's chair. For a second, as Stella let the invisible hands lower her into it, something in her face kept Dusty feeling sorry for her. And then, looking past her, he saw Jan, dancing with Dan Rogan, and was only sorry for himself.

They stopped beside the table. Scrambling up to his feet Dusty wished they hadn't. He hated to see Dan Rogan looking at Jan with that smirk on his rattrap mouth, and he was worried, too, for fear Jan might hurt his chance of holding Rick in line. The way Rick felt about her almost anything she said or did might rub him the wrong way.

She split a smile neatly between him and Dusty and made up a fresh one, a little different, for Stella. Her hello included them all, and Dusty guessed that it about averaged up the three different ways she felt toward them.

"Hiya, Red," Rick said. Dusty could tell he was trying to make her sore at him. "Fancy meeting the lower classes here, huh?"

Jan only laughed. That was good business, Dusty

told himself. Rick never could help softening up a little toward anybody who handed him a laugh on a wisecrack.

"It's Duss's party, but it'll be okay with him if you sit in. How about it?"

Jan hesitated, long enough for Rick's face to start freezing up again and for Dusty to be afraid she was going to refuse. That was what Rick was expecting, he knew. Rick didn't think there was any danger of Jan's joining a party that had Stella in it. He'd only asked her so that she'd turn him down and give him a chance to claim, afterward, that she had showed herself up as a snob and a phoney, had proved that all her friendliness toward Dusty had been just an act to kid him into working on her fire.

If that was his idea, it went wrong. Jan only laughed again and thanked him and sat down. He didn't look pleased about it, and neither did Dan Rogan. The smirk had rubbed itself off his mouth and his eyes were paler than ever as they slid sidewise toward Stella, but there wasn't anything for him to do but to follow Jan's lead. By the time, though, that the waiter had brought two more chairs and slithered away after two more cocktails the music started up again, and at the first note of it Rogan was on his feet, asking Stella to dance.

Dusty had to give him credit. He hadn't been able to keep Jan from sitting at the table, but he could take Stella away from it, and keep her away from it for most of the time Jan would be sitting there.

Rick stood up.

"Come on, Red. The boy-friend's gone native. You might as well do it too."

Jan's eyebrows pulled together, but only for a second. Then she gave him his laugh and got up. They were gone for quite a while, and there was time enough for Dusty to get lonesome and sorry for himself, and to do some worrying about their putting on a fight out there where he wouldn't be able to stop it. But when they came back Rick was laughing, and when Jan spoke about the fire he talked as if he meant to keep on with the job. Dusty breathed a little easier, but he wasn't very sorry when Jan and Rogan finished their drinks and went over to their own table.

Stella sent her lazy smile after them. She kept it on when she turned to Rick.

"Well, well! And I always thought you had a rule about girls like that! Or maybe—" she hesitated —"or maybe you don't think this one's like that, any more. Maybe——"

"Skip it," Rick said. "They're all like that." He gave Dusty a quick, sidelong look. "I steered the redhead away from Duss before she had time to do any work on him, that's all."

Stella took time to study him, her eyes half shut. Then they widened again, and there was something different in her smile. As if, Dusty thought, she had seen something that she liked.

"Oh, like that, eh? How I misjudged you! But how could I guess you were just staging a rescue act? You know so much about us Junior League girls that it never struck me you didn't have little Miss Lacy-pants spotted for a money player, like all the rest of us."

"What do you mean—I didn't have her spotted?" Rick's voice was sharp. "Didn't I just get through saying——?"

"You just got through saying you were afraid to give her a chance to work on Dusty." Stella laughed. "Dusty! When she's got Dan Rogan hanging on the ropes, ready for the kayo, and anybody can see it! Or maybe you didn't notice that. Maybe you didn't see how he looked when she sat in on our party, or what a hurry he was in to get me away from the table, so the air would be clean enough for Little Snowwhite! Or maybe you think she didn't notice it!"

She laughed again. Rick's eyes narrowed, for a moment, and then he joined in the laugh.

"She noticed, all right. She pretty near sprained her neck out there, trying to see whether you were pulling any presents off her Christmas tree."

He gave Dusty another sidewise look.

"It's no use carrying the torch, Duss. The redhead's a businesswoman. She sees a chance to clamp the ball and chain on Dan Rogan, and that's that. All you've got wouldn't even buy you a good going-over from her. We could lick her fire for her and all it would get you would be a few kind words and an orange. She doesn't know you're in the league."

Dusty was afraid that part of it was true. The

part about Jan's not knowing he was in the league, anyway. Maybe some of the rest of it was true, too. A girl could fall for Dan Rogan, easily enough, even a girl like Jan. It wouldn't be on account of his money, nor on account of all he was doing to help her out of the jam she was in, but neither of those things would hurt his chances much.

"You're telling Dusty?" Stella spoke up before Dusty could think of anything to say. "Right from the start he's been trying to tell you that she doesn't know he's alive. You're the one that worked out the bright idea that she was on his trail."

"You thought so, too," Rick said. "That night at Mink Schwartz's you said she——"

"Yes, angel." Stella said it with a sort of tired patience, as if she was talking to a thickheaded kid. "I did say she could go for Dusty. But I said it when I didn't know there was any white-haired papa in the picture, with a safe-deposit box full of swell reasons why she hadn't better go for anybody except Dan Rogan. You haven't heard me mention the idea since, have you?"

Rick took time to think. Stella flicked her eyes

toward Dusty. He guessed they were warning him to go on keeping his mouth shut. He would have done that anyway. He couldn't see why she should be rubbing it into him that he didn't stand much chance with Jan, but he knew she had a reason for doing it. And Rick knew that, too.

"So what?" His voice had a rasp in it.

Stella fitted a cigarette into a long, slim holder and lit it with the platinum lighter Rick had bought her after the Long Beach fire.

"So I'm wondering why you're afraid to go ahead with this job," she said. "It's one time when you've got Dan Rogan and World Pete working for you, instead of your working for them. If you put this fire out you don't just collect a few grand and let somebody else get the gravy. If there's any gravy, you get some of it, and you keep right on getting it. Of course there might not be much of it. That part of it's a gamble. But if you're afraid of a gamble it's certainly news."

Rick had to laugh at that one.

"So what?" he said again.

"So what's wrong with the proposition?" Stella

said. "Unless you're still afraid the redhead might pass up a few million bucks and glamor Dusty into giving you the air——"

She stopped. Rick's face was ugly. He didn't say anything, though, and after a minute she went on.

"I don't see what you're afraid of." She was repeating the word on purpose, Dusty knew, the way a bullfighter waves a red banner. "All you can lose is a few days' work, and when I think about the money you stand to win——" she waved the cigarette-holder in a wide, eloquent arc. Rick laughed harshly.

"When would you think about anything else, baby?" He laughed again. "Okay. Keep right on thinking. We'll play it your way."

Stella paid him off with the smile she saved up for extra-special thank-yous. Watching her, though, Dusty was a little puzzled. Considering the clever way she'd managed things she ought to be looking pleased with herself. And she didn't. It didn't make sense, but he couldn't help thinking that she was sorry about something. She looked just as she had looked when she was crooning that soppy torch-song about knowing all the answers but only knowing them by heart.

It didn't make sense, either, when Dusty ought to be sitting on top of the world over Rick's having agreed to go through with the job, for him to be having a sort of torch-song feeling of his own. But he got one, just the same, whenever he let his glance go across the dancing-space to Rogan's table.

Rick wasn't the only one to whom Stella had managed to sell the idea that there wasn't much danger of Jan Morel's turning down Dan Rogan for the sake of a big, dumb redneck named Dusty Miller.

8

DAN ROGAN stopped his car well back from the fire. Ahead of him, where a World Petroleum crew was unloading a big caterpillar crane from the trailer that had rushed it up from Bayou Rouge, he saw Big Jim Hafey turn and, after a moment, come slouching back toward him. He waited, his teeth showing. One of the good things about playing fairy godfather to the M-H Oil Company was that it permitted him to be seen in public with Jim Hafey. He was going to enjoy this interview, partly because Hafey was going to hate it.

There were other pleasures, though, to be had from the encounter. There was no need to keep any secrets from Hafey. In his company Rogan could drop all pretense and be himself. He could take the careful wrappings off his wits and exhibit them for exactly what they were. He could indulge himself, without penalty, in the stupid man's luxury of showing off, bragging. That his listener was unwilling and hostile only added relish to the process for him.

Hafey stopped beside the car. His plump, brick-colored face was smoothly expressionless, except for the narrowing of his eyes. Their lower lids, habitually lifted to the rim of the iris in the permanent squint of men who spend their lives in naked country and fierce sun, were higher, now; there was barely room enough above them for Hafey's eyes to peep out, wary, suspicious.

"Well? What's the idea? Shake your sleeve."

Even this far from the fire he had to lift his voice, but no one could have overheard him if he had shouted. The roar of the fire swallowed lesser noises. It built an invisible soundproof wall around them.

Rogan liked that. It was a pleasant change to be free to yell at Hafey if he wanted to. Up to now he had talked to him, when he risked talking to him at all, in canny, guarded undertones.

"I should think even you could guess the answer to that one, Hafey. The idea is to get this fire out."

Hafey grunted.

"If I didn't know better I'd almost think you meant it."

"Then you'd spoil a perfect record by guessing right, for once." Rogan uncovered two more teeth. "Of course I mean it."

Hafey laughed heavily.

"Sure. That's why you offered Farren and Miller double money on your Bayou Rouge job—just to make sure they'd stay here and go after ours, instead!"

"My dear Hafey!" Rogan wagged his head compassionately, "don't you see that I had to make that offer. I'm working for World Petroleum. I——"

"That's what World Pete thinks!" Hafey said.

"Exactly." Rogan kept on showing the teeth. "As you say, that is what World Pete thinks. And what would World Pete think if I hadn't done my best, ostensibly, to hire Farren and Miller for our job? I had to go through the motions of trying to get them, but you surely can't believe I'm sorry they turned me down."

"Why not?" Hafey was shaken but still skeptical.

"Oh, use what little intelligence you've got!" Rogan's patience wore suddenly thin. "What's in it for me, personally, if this fire finishes breaking you and Morel? I may get orders to buy in the pieces for World Petroleum, fire and all, but if so I'll have to buy them cheap, won't I? So cheap that you won't have anything to divide with me, afterward. But suppose the fire's out before you go broke? In that case the property won't be on the market. There won't be any reason—any visible reason, I mean—why you should sell your interest in it. So, if I manage to persuade you to sell it to my esteemed employers, they won't criticize me for paying you a fairly stiff price—stiff enough to make it pleasant for both of us when we split it up. See?"

Hafey thought it over.

"There's one thing I don't see," he said. "I don't

see how you're going to square yourself for this big-hearted way you're helping us off the spot. How are you going to alibi yourself for spending World Pete dough on——"

"Not spending, Hafey." Rogan laughed silently. "Lending. Don't worry about my alibi. If I should need one it's on file in advance. But I shan't need one. My revered superiors at headquarters already understand what I'm doing and heartily approve of it." He went through the motions of another noiseless laugh. "You may not have noticed that there hasn't been any agreement as to what our charges will be for the help we're giving you. Your company already owes World Petroleum quite a bill, Hafey, and I'm afraid it's going to be a great deal bigger. Even with your fire out you might have a little difficulty finding the money to settle with us. And in that event——" he shrugged his shoulders and spread his hands.

"In that event you put on the screws and World Pete takes over the whole proposition."

"It's possible," Rogan said. "Even probable, perhaps."

"And if we lick the fire, you strongarm me into selling my stock to World Pete and then shake me down for the hog's share of what I get for it."

"You put it coarsely but accurately," Rogan said.

Hafey took time to think.

"All you want from me is all I've got, the same as usual. And all you want from Frank Morel is all he's got." He stopped. "Including his kid, maybe?"

"We'll leave Miss Morel out of it." Rogan's smile had frozen; the smooth silkiness of his voice was a little colder still. Neither of these things, however, seemed to impress Hafey.

"That was just my idea," he said. "The kid's out. She stays out. All the way. I'm telling you, Rogan."

"Telling me?" Rogan's eyebrows went up. "I don't think I like that, Hafey. In the circumstances it seems as if I'm the one to do the telling. You——"

"I'm doing it this time, and if you're as smart as you think you are, you're listening. The kid's out. Or else."

"Or else what?" The eyebrows stayed up. "Aren't you overlooking that little matter of——?"

"You might be overlooking something yourself,"

Hafey said. "You might be forgetting that even a top hand can be overplayed."

"I'm not worried about overplaying mine," Rogan said.

"It's a good one, all right," Hafey admitted. "There's only one way it can lose."

Rogan shook his head. "Not even that many."

"That's what you think. Take a look at this." Hafey lifted a puffy finger to his windpipe. "See this here neck? Well, any time you catch yourself figuring Morel's kid in as part of your take, just remember it's all the neck I've got and ask yourself how many hangin's it's good for."

"I don't think there's much danger of your asking for even the first one," Rogan said.

"Maybe there ain't. But then again, if a man's the kind that can see red enough to forget he's taking chances on a neck-knot, he might be the kind that could see just as red again sometime. Maybe you're safe in betting on me staying scared of hangin' number one, Rogan, but don't go betting too heavy on it. And don't bet a nickel on me ever being scared of hangin' number two."

Without waiting for Rogan to speak, he swung around and lumbered back toward the fire. For a few moments Rogan sat still, his face smoothed to the blankness that meant his wits were hard at work. They did not find him any convincing answer, though, for the doctrine that no hand is too high to be overplayed. When he faced Jan Morel, up where the big caterpillar was feeling its way down the skids from the low-slung trailer, he carefully greeted her with only the affable brevity of a man too intent upon urgent affairs of business to spare time or thought on anything outside of them.

9

THROUGH dark glasses the fire looked almost as bright as without them, but the sky, even where the floating mountain of smoke didn't hide it, was browny-black, the way it looked when a dust-storm was blowing down from the Bowl. Jan was used to that, by now, and used to the screaming roar, so that she only heard it when she thought about it. But there were things she didn't get used to.

She didn't get used to standing back, outside of an invisible and yet impassable wall of heat, and watching men, helmeted and grotesquely bloated in their asbestos suits, like deep-sea divers, and like divers, too, in their labored heaviness of movement, inching up to swirling gusts and spouts and rolling waves of flame, heavy hoses shooting streams of water at their backs, water that exploded into steam when it spattered on the metal shield they pushed ahead of them. Instead of getting easier to take, this was harder, every time she watched it.

And she had to watch. Not watching was even worse. There had been plenty of chances, during a desperate week, for her to find that out. Most of the tangle of twisted wreckage had been cleared away, fished out by patient grapplings in a giant, nightmare game of jackstraws. Every piece of it had cost at least one of those crazy journeys in close to the heart of the fire; more often than not the pain and toil and danger went for nothing and the two men would come stumbling back, beaten, spent, stifling, to breathe and rest and try again. It was hateful enough to stand looking on, shamefully safe, but it was more bearable than turning her back and waiting.

Guthead Marr stopped beside her. He leaned down to shout into her ear.

"Get that chin up, Red." He'd been calling her Red ever since he'd heard Rick Farren do it. The queer thing was that she hated Rick a little harder every time he used the name and yet liked to have Guthead use it. "They got it licked."

Jan tried to believe it. But it didn't look to her as if the fire was much nearer to being licked than when they'd started on it. In spite of all the wreckage they'd cleared away the flames were shooting out just about as far and flatly as ever, with only a few breaks, narrow and wavering, in the solidness of them.

Something in her face must have told Guthead how she felt. He yelled down at her again.

"I'm tellin' yuh, Red. All they gotta do is snake that crown-block outa there and this time they're gonna get it. After that it's a pushover for them two guys."

Jan kept on trying to believe it. That was getting harder and harder to do, even when it was Dusty who was telling her. There were five tons of whitehot steel in the giant pulley they called the crown-block. They'd had four tries at getting a hitch on it and dragging it away from where it had crashed down on the casing-head. Maybe this time, though, they were going to do it.

She went forward into the heat. Dusty and some World Pete men were working over a light wire-line, their backs toward her. Rick Farren, an unlighted cigarette pasted to his underlip, stood looking on. Jan could tell that he was keyed up, impatient, the way he always was, with the dull business of being careful and the tameness of taking pains. He came toward her, scowling.

"Roll your hoop, will you?" It was queer how easily his voice got through the bedlam roar. "You can't do yourself any good out here, nor anybody else. Go on up in the grandstand. You can see all you need from there."

Jan moved a hand to tell him she wanted to see Dusty. His face got a little uglier. It had been doing that, more and more, every time she came near Dusty.

"Yeah. I know. But you don't have to work on

him right now. You got him sold. He'll go in there for you without any more handling. Scram, will you, and let us get on the job?"

Jan couldn't have made him hear her even if arguing would have done any good. She was turning away when Dusty looked around and saw her. He came over to her.

"All set." He shouted it. His teeth showed but Jan knew it wasn't a real grin. She had found out that Dusty didn't get any kick out of going in there.

"Relax." He cupped his hand around the shout. "It's in the bag."

It was the same thing he'd said the other times, but there was something different about it, now. Always before she had got the idea that it was himself that he was trying to convince. This time he didn't seem to be thinking about his side of it; all he wanted to do was to make her side of it, the waiting and the watching, a little easier.

It wouldn't have been any use trying to make him hear her, even if she had known what it was that she wanted to say. All she could do was to join her hands, hooking the fingers together, and move them quickly up and down in front of her. Somehow the imitation of a handshake seemed to carry a meaning that a real one couldn't have carried. Dusty seemed to feel the same way about it. He gave it back to her, anyhow; and there was more realness, this time, about his grin.

He turned back to his work. Jan stood and watched for a little while. Then there was a nudge at her arm and she looked up to find Rick Farren giving her his narrow grin and jerking a thumb toward the plank road. His voice came through the uproar of the fire.

"There's Rogan's bus, Red. Go fry yourself some fish."

Jan went. She was getting hardened to hearing him say such things. She hardly resented them any more. She could even make allowances for his thinking them. Dusty had made her understand that Rick really thought all women were like the kind he had known, Stella Conway's kind, cold-blooded, shifty, scheming gold-diggers. It was logical enough for him to see a selfish reason behind Jan's friendliness with a man as useful to her as Dan Rogan, and it was just as logical for him to believe the friendliness must be counterfeit, hating Rogan as he did, with that blind, senseless male hatred in which Frank Morel and Jim Hafey and Dusty Miller mysteriously shared. It just wasn't possible for him to believe that Jan could honestly like the man, honestly admire and respect and trust him, honestly take comfort, as she took it now, in his nearness.

She hurried a little. In whipcords and riding-boots Rogan managed to look as starched and laundered as in white linens, and as cool, in spite of the blistering heat. That immaculacy and coolness, where ordinary men were grimed and sweating, always seemed to Jan a proof of Rogan's extraordinariness. They confirmed the poised, confident carriage of his compact body, the calm self-certainty that looked at her out of his eyes.

That self-assurance gave her, now, a sudden, grateful defense against anxiety. Nothing that Dan Rogan didn't want to happen, she thought, would dare to happen where those steel-colored eyes could see it.

"I'm so glad you could come out, Dan. I don't do so much worrying when you're here."

He looked pleased, but he shook his head.

"There's nothing for you to worry about," he said. "Everything's going to be all right." He slipped a hand in the bend of her elbow, guiding her back along the plank road. There was steel in the touch and Jan's confidence took strength from it. But when they stopped and sat on a pile of lumber her face manifestly wasn't confident enough to please Rogan.

"Stop worrying, I tell you." His voice had authority, command. "We're going to put it out."

"The fire?" Jan almost laughed. "I wasn't thinking about that. It's—it's those two boys."

She glanced, half unwillingly, toward the new shack, over by the new water-well and pumps. Rick and Dusty were rolling the mud of the sump, as they always did before they put on the asbestos suits. They had looked funny, she remembered, the first time she'd watched them doing this.

"Of course," Rogan said. "But you needn't worry about them, either. They're working at their trade and they're good at it. They're even better than I thought, and I always had them rated pretty high.

They're so good that they really aren't in much danger, out there."

Jan's heart warmed toward him. Instinct told her that he didn't like Rick and Dusty, but he didn't let his dislike color his opinion of their ability. He was just to them, and even generous, whenever he spoke of them.

"I used to think they got by mainly on luck, before I watched them working on this job of yours," he went on. "I still think they're lucky, but it's a pretty special kind of luck—the kind that doesn't happen to people who don't earn it. Those two earn it. They're good, both of them, but when they work together they're better than good. They team up better than any other pair I ever saw or hope to see. They coordinate like one person with four arms and four legs—and a first-rate brain giving all eight their orders."

Jan nodded. She had watched that queerly perfect teamplay and wondered at it. Sometimes, unreasonably, she had felt something like resentment toward it. She even resented it now, a little, in spite of knowing that Rogan was right in thinking it would take some of the danger out of what Rick and Dusty would be doing, out there, in a few minutes.

"They even team up mentally," he was saying. "Farren hasn't any real intelligence, for instance, but what wits he has work instantly, like an animal's. Miller has plenty of brains, but they think slowly. Farren probably doesn't know what it feels like to be afraid. Miller's too intelligent not to be afraid—of the things any rational man ought to be afraid of. Farren's a born gambler and Miller would never take a chance if he could get his way without it. Without Farren out in front of him he'd never go near a fire, and without Miller holding him down Farren would have gone too close to one a long time ago. Between them they strike a sort of average that takes them in just far enough and gets them out alive. That's why they've put out all those other fires and why I'm betting on them to put this one out for you."

The last sentence jarred on Jan's ear. Everything he had said was true, and she ought to be glad that it was true. But there was something wrong, somewhere, with the way he said it. Almost, she thought, as if he were talking about a football game, or a fight or a horserace. Almost as if, except for having bet on it, he wouldn't be much interested in how it turned out.

Some hint of the idea must have shown itself in her look. Usually he was good at reading her face, but he was wrong about it this time. He took the faint frown as a sign that he hadn't yet convinced her.

"It's all right, I tell you. Look over there." He nodded toward his car, chuckling. "There's somebody who isn't doing any worrying. Somebody with plenty to lose, too."

Jan's glance went by him, and her anger went by him with it, instantly shifting to the woman who sat on the running-board, silken legs generously crossed, compact open, lipstick painstakingly at work on carefully flattened mouth. It would have been cold-blooded enough for any woman to be doing that. For Stella Conway to be doing it, with Rick Farren's emerald blinking on her finger——

She must have felt the burn of Jan's eyes. She turned her head, anyway, and waved the lipstick, a slow, insolently travestied salute. Jan gave her back half an inch of nod and looked away, not too quickly.

"See?" Rogan said. "She isn't worried about the fire. She isn't even interested in it. She's watched Farren work on too many others. She knows he's perfectly safe—out there. What she wants to know is—" he chuckled again—"is how safe he is in here."

"Here?" Jan was bewildered.

"With you," Rogan said. There was a thin amusement in his voice. "She's been away for three or four days and she's been hearing things. It seems you've been on a few parties with Farren, and——"

Jan couldn't help laughing.

"She can't possibly be stupid enough to think—why, she can't help knowing Rick hates me! The only reason he came along with Dusty and me those two evenings we went dancing was because he knew I was hoping he wouldn't! He——"

Rogan lifted a hand. He was still palely amused. "I know. I think she does, too. There's nothing stupid about her. She just likes to be sure."

Jan had stopped listening. The two helmeted figures were moving toward the fire, pushing a wheeled shield ahead of them, a light wireline trailing out behind. The hose was sending a bright arc of water at their backs.

"They're going to do it this time," Rogan said.

Jan wished he wouldn't talk. He was saying what she wanted to hear, wanted to believe, but there was still something wrong with the way he said it. There was something wrong with her sitting here beside him. The grandstand . . . Rick's word found a sudden meaning, and somehow Rogan fitted himself into that meaning. That was what was wrong. He was just a spectator, watching a good show. She didn't belong here with him in a grandstand seat. She belonged——

Against her will something turned her head so that she was looking at Stella. One of Stella's hands still held the compact up in front of her and the other one was dabbing the lipstick at her mouth. But this time Jan wasn't fooled. That was where she belonged. Over on that running-board with some one else who wasn't watching horses run or boys play games. She jumped down, half running.

"It's going to be all right, Stella." She hadn't

meant to say the name, and she could see that Stella didn't thank her for doing it. There was a hard enmity in the look that lifted to meet hers. She went on, though. "Dan Rogan says——"

"I know what he says." Stella's drawl was wearily bitter. "He's been telling me, all the way out here. Everything's going to be just dandy. The boys are going to slap your fire down for you and Dan Rogan's going to make a barrel of money out of it——"

"He didn't say that, did he?" Jan spoke quickly. "It isn't true. He hasn't any interest in this lease. He——"

"He didn't need to say it. Any time Dan Rogan licks his chops and purrs it means somebody's making money for him. Like Rick's doing, out there. Like he'll be doing again, in a little while, down at Bayou Rouge, if he gets by this job alive! He——"

She stopped. Her face stiffened. Jan turned to follow the direction of the suddenly changed look. Instantly she forgot about everything else but the two swollen figures, moving straight into the wall of fire.

For a few seconds that stretched out into little lifetimes she lost sight of them. Then she could see them again. Coming back. She could catch in a breath, a deep one, all the way down. Something was hurting the inside of her hand. A wrist. Stella's. She had to try twice before she could let go of it.

One of the figures waved an arm.

"They've got hold of it," she heard herself saying. "Dusty said he'd wave if they did. It's—it's all right."

"Yes. Till next time." Stella's voice was still hard. Jan noticed that her hands, fiddling with the compact, were shaking a little.

"It'll be different next time," she said. "They won't be walking through the fire when they go in again. As soon as they drag that crown-block away from——"

She didn't finish the sentence. A caterpillar was snailing away from the fire, barely moving, lifting the wireline. Jan's nerves could feel the tension on the thin steel thread. She had forgotten about breathing, again. If the line held——

There was a sudden change in fire, a break in its

solid front. A wedge-shaped gap, reaching in to the center of it, narrow and wavering.

"They've done it!" She was pointing at the cleft, trying to believe it was wide enough to serve, trying, at any rate, to sound and look as if she believed it was. "Dusty was right! All they had to do was to move that block. They can—they can go in there, now, and——"

"And take some nitroglycerine along." Stella stood up. She smoothed down her skirt, deliberately, over her hips. "Even Rick wouldn't have tried that before, but he'll try it now, all right. It's just the nice, safe, sure-thing kind of a gamble he goes for."

Her eyes met Jan's. There wasn't any expression in them, nor in her voice.

"Don't look so worried, Lacypants. He'll get by with it. This is just the kind of a bet he wins. He'll get that can of soup all the way in and be out again before it pops. Your fire'll be out and you'll own a gold-mine and everything'll be just swell. Till the next time."

"There won't be any next time," Jan said. "If they put this fire out——"

"There's another one, waiting for them, down at Bayou Rouge. And there'll be plenty more, after that."

"Rick and Dusty won't be fighting them," Jan said.

"Won't they?" Stella said. "Why not?"

"Why should they?" Jan said. "They'll have more money than they can spend, if they——"

"Rick won't spend any of his share buying brains," Stella said. "He'll be doing this to me till——"

She stopped. For a moment her face had been awake and passionate. There was nothing in it now but the hard coolness that was usually in it. Her eyes went by Jan.

"All right, Dan. Let's go."

Jan turned. Rogan was just behind her. He looked pleased. She told herself angrily that it was the way he ought to look. There was every generous reason why he should be glad that Rick and Dusty hadn't been hurt, that they'd made a real start, at last, toward putting out the fire. It was contemptible of her, and stupid and thankless, to be thinking that Stella had been right about that small, pale, satisfied smile of his, to be telling herself that he did look as if he were licking his chops.

"You aren't going, are you, Dan?" No matter how he looked she wanted him to stay.

"I'm afraid I must." He seemed to read her thought. The smile changed a little. "I'm sorry. I'd certainly like to be here and watch the boys blow this one out."

"Do you think they're going to?" She watched his eyes. There was just a chance that they might tell her whether he was giving an honest answer or trying to comfort her with a kindly lie.

"Of course they're going to! There's nothing to it now. This is all those two needed, and more. You practically owe them their piece of your lease right now."

She couldn't help believing him. Some of her anxiety was lifted. She could smile back at him. She could even laugh.

"You're wrong, for once. I don't owe it to them."

His eyebrows went up.

"They've got their stock already," she said. "I gave it to them before they started."

He kept on staring. She laughed again. There was something funny about finding out that he could be astonished, like ordinary people.

"Don't look so shocked," she said. "I didn't have any choice about it. I had to do business with Rick Farren, and he just wasn't doing it on faith. Not with me. I'm a woman."

Rogan nodded. The pleased look had come back. It puzzled Jan a little, this time. She hadn't said anything to put that sudden, relishing complacency into his face.

The look seemed to interest Stella, too. Jan glanced at her. She was studying Rogan with a queer, considering intentness, a thoughtful puckering at the corners of her eyes.

"Well, you certainly took a long chance," Rogan said, "but——"

"What was long about it?" Stella's voice sounded a little sharp. "When did Rick ever gyp you on a finger bet? You or anybody else you know about?"

"I'm sorry." Rogan lifted a hand, palm outward. "I didn't mean anything like that. I just meant that it wasn't exactly businesslike, that's all. And anyway it doesn't matter. They've got it licked!" He turned to Jan. "Stop worrying, Jan. It's all over but the shouting."

He made her ashamed of having let a doubt of him get into her mind, even for the little time it had stayed there.

"If it is, I've got you to thank for it," she said. "If it hadn't been for you——"

"Forget it." He made a brushing gesture. "And stop worrying. It's all right, I tell you. They'll blow it out the first shot. I'm only sorry I can't stay and see them do it."

He moved toward the car and stopped, snapping his fingers.

"There! I almost forgot! Sorry, Stella, but I'll have to keep you waiting a few minutes. I've got to see McGoorty."

Stella made a carelessly assenting motion with the fingers of her left hand. Her eyes were still narrowed as they watched him going over toward the new shacks. Jan turned and watched him, too. She saw him nod and wave a hand to Big Jim Hafey as they passed each other, and noticed disapprovingly that Big Jim barely acknowledged the gesture. Rogan went on to the pump-shed, talked to Ed McGoorty for a few moments and started back. Stella got into the car. Jan discovered suddenly that she was sorry about that.

"I wish you wouldn't go," she said. "It—it helped, having you here. Why don't you stay and——?"

"Not me," Stella said. Her lipstick was at work again and her carefully warped mouth made the words sound blurry. "I've seen fires before, and they're all pretty much alike. I'd be waiting around all day before there's any more excitement, and——"

"Don't," Jan said. "You aren't fooling me."

Stella looked at her, over the top of the compact.

"This must be one of my off days," she said. "I don't even seem to be fooling myself—much."

"You are if you think it's easier to take when you aren't watching it," Jan said. "It isn't. It's harder. You know it's happening and you don't know——"

"Skip it," Stella said. She lifted her voice a little. It was itself again, lazy and light and flippant. "I should stick around here looking at fireworks and pass up a chance to go buggy-riding with—" she laughed—"with World Pete! Come on, Dan. Let's go."

Jan turned. Rogan was just behind her. If he had heard what Stella said his face didn't show what he thought about it.

"It's all right, Jan. They've got it licked. I'm sorry I won't be here to see the finish, but it can't be helped. I'll give you a ring tonight."

He slid in behind the wheel without waiting for her to answer. Stella waved good-bye with the lip-stick as the car started turning, the same exagger-ated, almost mocking gesture she had used before. But this time Jan didn't resent it. In spite of that sudden change back into hard-boiledness and flip-pancy, she kept right on liking Stella.

Dusty and Rick and some other men were busy, over by the shacks. She couldn't see what they were doing and started toward them to find out. Before she'd gone half way, though, Dusty looked around and saw her. He lifted an arm and motioned her to go back. She could see he was in earnest about it. She stopped and waited while he came toward her. When he was near enough for her to see his face it was grinning, but not quite cheerfully enough to satisfy her.

"What's the matter? Why can't I——?"

"You're plenty near enough, right here." He mopped sweat off his face with the back of his hand. "We're fixing up a little surprise package for your fire. Forty quarts of soup. Go on back."

Jan shot a quick look toward the fire. The dent in it looked narrower, suddenly.

"No! You're not going to do it. Not for all the oil there is!"

He blinked at her.

"Why not? There's nothing to it. We just——"

"You just try to walk through that fire, pushing forty quarts of nitroglycerine ahead of you! To save me some money! To——"

"Who? Me?" He laughed. "Do I look that crazy? We only hauled the crown-block a little way from where it was. It's still right in there and we've got a line to it, and we've got a crack in the fire, too. All we do is hoist up our end of the line and let the can of soup slide down it through the crack till it hits the block. Whango! Where did that fire go?"

"Is that all?" Jan said. "Honestly?"

He made a crossmark over his heart.

"Will it work?"

"It will if——" he stopped.

"If what?"

"If it works." He grinned. "If we didn't haul the block too far. If the soup doesn't blow before it's all the way in. If the gas doesn't reignite from that busted b.o.p. and casing. That's my main worry. They're pretty hot. But we've got a good chance. You go back where you came from and keep your fingers crossed."

He held up his own. Jan imitated them with hers. He started back, stopped, after a few steps, and turned.

"Be sure and open your mouth when you see the can start in."

She nodded and waved her hand. She felt cheerful, walking back to the pile of lumber. She didn't even seem to mind the waiting, now, although there was plenty of it to do. It was a long, long time before she saw the boom of the big caterpillar-crane go up, lifting a shining spiderweb thread of wire.

Just in time, as the canister of nitro went sliding down toward the fire, she remembered to open her mouth.

A solid wall of air pushed her back against the lumber and the world was nothing but a noise. Something lifted the whole mass of the fire and tossed it upward, coherent, like something that had substance, against the black ceiling of the smoke. It hung there, for a long instant, like a balloon, and then, disintegrating into little tattered rags of flame, it was gone.

There was a difference in the roar, now, that made it good to hear, instead of hateful. The angry, screaming sound was gone. There was time for Jan Morel to draw in one long, deep happy breath.

If only those pieces of broken steel weren't too hot! If only——

Through the blot of nitro smoke above the crater, she saw a little stab of light. She heard, a thousand times more hateful than before, the screeching snarl of fire, and watched the giant toadstool of flame spring up again.

10

By the time Dusty reached the supply shed, back of the pumps, Rick was just starting to dress.

"What's the idea?" Dusty said. Rick looked up from the white-silk sock he was pulling on. His eyes were like black glass buttons.

"The idea is Beauport. I'm taking time out while you think up a few more bright ideas. Get moving if you're coming with me."

Dusty could see he was keyed up, but not the way he would have been if they'd killed the fire; he was like a drunk, halfway to the top, about at the fighting stage.

"You go ahead," he said. "I'd better ride in with Jan. She'll be pretty sunk."

"Yeah," Rick said. "And of course that's all we got to do—keep the redhead happy! It'd be just too bad if she had to do her worrying by herself, for a change."

Dusty kept his mouth shut. It had been a mistake to say anything about Jan. Rick would have been grouchy enough over their failure to put out the fire; talking about Jan was like rubbing salt into a blister. Rick acted uglier every time her name was mentioned. She'd gone out of her way to be nice to him; but it only seemed to make him sorer at her, and sorer at Dusty for spending some of his time with her. He'd got it into his head that she was making a sap of Dusty, stringing him along just for the fun of it, and it was no use trying to tell him that she wasn't. The two or three times when Dusty had gone around to the old house in the evening instead of helling around with Rick at nightspots like Mink Schwartz's, Rick had talked about quitting the job. Dusty could see that he was almost sore enough, now, to do it.

"Go ahead," Rick said. "Speak your piece. Maybe I'll fall for it again." He mimicked Dusty's voice. "This is our big chance to throw the harpoon into Rogan and make him like it!" He sawed off a laugh. "You sold me that one once. I might go for it again."

"Why not? What's wrong with it?"

"I'll tell you what's wrong with it. You were playing me for a sucker. All that build-up about Rogan was just a bill of goods. You never gave a damn about Rogan or anything else except doing yourself some good with the redhead! What do you care if we pass up the biggest piece of dough we ever got a crack at? What do you care if we put in a couple of weeks working on this fire for a pocketful of bird-seed, as long as it helps you make a play for high-snoot dame who'd wipe her feet after stepping on you!"

Dusty had to take a fresh grip on his temper.

"Let's leave Jan out of it," he said. "You know why I wanted to take on this job. It was our chance to gamble for something worth gambling for—for the chance to quit taking chances. Quit for keeps. That's the only gamble that ever looked good to me or ever will. If we lick this fire, we never need to look at another one. We——"

"I know," Rick said. "We can park ourselves back of a couple of glass-topped desks and live happy ever afterwards."

"That wasn't my idea," Dusty said, "but at that we might do worse. We might keep right up the way we are, fooling around fires for easy money and feeding it to deserving guys like Mink Schwartz, and——"

"Why don't you pull the one about the gold spittoons?" Rick said. "You got the rest of the speech right where that came from."

"I might think up a few things myself," Dusty said.

"Sure you might. But you never did, up to a couple of weeks ago. Up to then there was no squawk about how we were doing. It's only since you went overboard for the redhead."

"We're leaving her out," Dusty said.

"Okay. She's out. But let's get it straight about what happens if we lick this job and it pays off in telephone numbers, like you hope. We settle down, do we, and be big business-men?"

"We sit in the real game," Dusty said. "The one I came out here to get into. We develop this lease. We put down a flock of wells. We——"

"We grow up into a couple of Dan Rogans." Rick was all dressed. He stopped in the doorway and looked back. "So that's what we're shooting at, huh?"

"We grow up, anyhow," Dusty said.

It was a little while before Rick spoke.

"Maybe you do," he said. His voice made Dusty look up quickly from the shoe he was tying, but Rick's face didn't tell him anything. It was more deadpan than ever, and the eyes in it were more than ever like black glass buttons. They met Dusty's for a second. Then Rick turned and went out.

Dusty finished dressing. He didn't like the way Rick had looked and sounded, but he wasn't really worried. Rick would see the job through, no matter how he felt about Jan. It wasn't in him to quit.

Jan and Jim Hafey were standing by the parked cars when Dusty came out of the shack.

Dusty went over to them. He felt a little better when Jan turned and flashed a smile at him.

"Tough luck, Duss," Jan said. "Your idea's all

right, though. I was just offering to bet Jim that it'll work the next time."

"There won't be any next time," Dusty said. "And you'd lose your bet if there was. It's no use blowing the fire out till we can cut off that split casing so the fire can shoot up straight. The way it is the gas'll keep right on catching fire again, just way it did this time."

"Cut off the casing?" Hafey shot a look over his shoulder at the fire. "Just how are you going to stay in there long enough to do it?"

"That's what I've got to figure out," Dusty said.

Hafey grunted and turned away. Dusty didn't blame him for being sunk and showing it. Even as good a loser as Big Jim had a right to do a little glooming in a case like this. He turned to Jan. What he saw in her eyes troubled him.

"Don't let it get you down," he said. "This is just another bad break. We'll get a good one any minute."

"Yes. I know." She pulled her mouth into a smile, but it looked as if she had a little trouble doing it. "Come on. Let's get away from here."

She went toward the Pierce, walking fast. Dusty

knew how she felt. Even when you were so used to it that you didn't know you were hearing it, the noise of a fire kept sawing into your brain. He wanted to get away from it himself. His nerves began easing down the minute the car started.

Jan didn't seem to feel like talking. That suited Dusty. Talking stirred your mind up, kept it thinking. And thinking let things into your head that you were trying to keep out of it. The fire, and the odds against your licking it. Dan Rogan, and the way he looked at Jan, and all the reasons there were for him to have a right to look at her like that. Rick. The snarl in his voice, and the soreness under the snarl. If there was no talk, if there was nothing but the drumming tires and the racketing old engine, you could put off thinking, for a while, about anything except the green cotton-rows, bright against the red earth, the scrub woods, drowsing, sundrenched, the low skyline, blessedly clean; the girl behind the big steering-wheel.

They'd driven quite a few miles before Jan spoke.

"You're wrong about the blonde of Rick's. I like her."

"I like her myself, kind of," Dusty said, "but I'm not wrong about her. She doesn't give anybody any chance to be wrong about her. She might as well carry a sign-board. On the make, every minute of every day. A hundred per cent for Stella, and she doesn't care who knows it. She'll tell Rick to his face that she gets a cut on what he loses in Mink Schwartz's, and the other day when he bought her that diamond clip she collected her rake-off from Guldenberg right in front of him, cool as a fish on ice."

Jan thought it over.

"And Rick loves it," she said.

"Sure he does. It checks up with all his pet ideas about women, and he likes that. And it keeps him from really falling for her, too, and that makes him feel it's safe to play around with her."

Jan laughed softly.

"Yes. So he keeps on playing around with her. I knew she was clever but I never guessed till today how crazy she is about Rick."

"She isn't," Dusty said. "She's crazy about a girl named Stella Conway and nobody else."

"You're wrong," Jan said. "I saw her face when she watched Rick going out toward that fire and it wasn't herself that she was thinking about."

"Don't let her fool you," Dusty said. "The only time she isn't thinking about herself is when she isn't thinking."

"Then she wasn't thinking, back there," Jan said. "She didn't look as if she was. She looked as if she was just—just dying a little. The way I was. The way I do every time I have to watch you—" she stopped and went on quickly—"you and Rick going in there."

Dusty didn't say anything. She didn't mean it the way it sounded, of course. But it sounded good.

"It gets worse every time," she said. "When I think of letting you do it again——"

"It'll only be once more. We won't go in there again till we've figured out how to——"

"Don't let's talk about it," she interrupted. "Right now I don't seem able to take even that." She flashed a quick smile at him. "Let's pretend there's nothing to think about but the juleps Zenie's going to give us when we get home and nothing to decide but whether we'll have supper on the gallery or go out and——"

"That's easy," Dusty said. "On the gallery." Just the thought of it rested him, and thinking about it seemed somehow to shorten the ride. He was almost startled, presently, when the car swerved into the drive under the magnolias and stopped in front of the old house. It didn't seem, now, to have any trouble about remembering where it had seen him before.

The gallery was dim and cool. There was thick frost on the tall silver tumblers that Zenie brought. The split-bamboo shades sliced the late sunlight into friendliness and a small breeze stirred the leaves of the wisteria that drooped from the latticed railing of the gallery overhead. Leaning back in the grateful sag of a basket-work chair, looking out of half-shut eyes at Jan, it wasn't very hard for Dusty to keep on forgetting about the things he didn't want to remember.

"It's a funny thing," he said, "but this house always makes me think of the one I used to live in."

"Why is it funny?" Jan said.

"Because there couldn't be any two houses much less alike. Or any two towns less alike than this one and Grimfield. And yet I keep feeling as if—well, there is something here that used to be up there. It isn't in any of the other oil towns."

"Oldness?" Jan suggested.

"Maybe. But that isn't all of it."

He could shut his eyes and see the two rows of prim white houses facing each other under the elms of the village green. Their serenity was utterly different from the drowsy peacefulness here, and yet it was somehow woven into one pattern with it in his thought.

"A kind of belongingness," he said. "People living where they were meant to live. The way they were meant to. And that's funny, too. That's what I used to hate, back there—feeling as if I was putting down roots, like a tree."

"I know," Jan said. "I used to feel that way, too. As if this was a cage I had to get out of. Whenever Dad talked about striking it rich all I ever thought about was New York and Palm Beach and Bar Harbor."

She laughed.

"But that was before there was any danger of our

not being able to stay here. It only needed that to make me realize I don't want to live anywhere else ever, or any other way."

"I shouldn't think you would," Dusty said. "That's what I've kept thinking ever since we stopped here, that first night. That you were dead right when you said you were gambling for something that was worth winning. I don't blame you for thinking this is worth gambling for, or anything else you have to do to keep on living here. I'd feel the same way about it if I belonged here."

He could feel that way, he discovered, even without belonging here. He could almost feel as if he did belong here and the feeling grew on him as Zenie brought them supper, and Jan kept him talking about Grimfield.

The more he told her about it the more it seemed to give him a kind of right to be here. That didn't make sense, but it was so. Worlds apart as they were, different in every possible way, there was something in common between Jan Morel and Aunt Effie. They were the same kind of people.

He kept getting surer of that as he told Jan about

Aunt Effie, and her fixed belief that no lady ever went outdoors without her bustle, and how the jet spikes on her black bonnet used to shiver when she was arguing with the two Misses Marple over what books ought to be barred from the Free Library and whether Ethan Littlefield, after donating two dollars to the Unitarians in the hope of getting the contract to repaint their church, had any right to call himself a Congregationalist, let alone wanting to be made an elder.

The sunlight paled into silver as they talked and ate. The night coolness slid in through the slatted shades. There was Mazagran coffee, and thimble glasses of brandy out of a dusty bottle.

This was it, Dusty kept thinking. The chance to live here, this way, to be sure of always doing it, was worth all Jan was risking to get it. Even a little sample of it, like this evening, was worth what Dusty was paying for it. Worth all the sweat and danger out there at Saragossa. Even worth having Rick sore at him.

Every now and then, though, Dusty couldn't help worrying a little about that. Three or four times he almost made up his mind to go hunt Rick up and try to smooth things over with him. But he always talked himself out of it. Very likely letting Rick alone was the quickest way of getting him over his grouch. Nightspotting around with Stella, hoisting a few drinks and dropping a little money, would take the kinks out of his nerves. Probably, feeling the way he did, he'd enjoy himself a lot better without Dusty around. It was dumb to keep feeling as if that talk, out at the lease, had been anything but talk, as if, just because Dusty wasn't there to stop him, Rick might do something that would——

The idea always stopped right there. That showed how dumb it was, Dusty told himself. There wasn't anything that Rick could do to hurt him, even if Rick had been the kind to want to hurt him. And Rick wasn't that kind.

Thinking about Rick, though, had let the fire get back into his mind. Against his will his wits were working on it. A way to saw through that casing when you couldn't stay within a hundred feet of it for more than a few seconds. A way to. . . .

"It doesn't make sense," Jan said. She sounded as

if she were talking to herself, but her voice took Dusty's thoughts away from unimportant things like burning oil-wells and brought them back to things that really mattered, like the queer feeling of belongingness. His tired body settled back contentedly into the friendly sag of the old basket-work chair.

"What doesn't?" he said.

"You," Jan said. "Me. Us. This." She waved her hand; the orange spark of her cigarette made an arc against the dusk. "Everything you've been telling me about yourself and your people and the way you were brought up ought to make me feel as if—as if——"

"As if I was some kind of a foreigner? Is that it?"

"Something like that. And it doesn't. It works just the other way. The more you talk about how different you and your people are from me and my people, the more it seems as if there wasn't any difference at all—none that matters, anyway."

"I know," Dusty said. "I've been wondering about that, too. I get the same feeling when you're telling me about things down here. I guess maybe the answer is that people aren't so different as they look, and the more you find out about 'em the more ways you find they're like each other. It's the places they live in that are different, not the people, except that the places make them different, on the outside, in ways that don't really amount to much."

"Perhaps that's it," Jan said.

"It's part of it, anyway. You take us Yankees. We've got the name of being closefisted, for instance. Maybe we rate it. But if we didn't have to scratch our living out of land that's half rocks, with maybe a hundred days between frosts, I guess it wouldn't be a great while before we could let go of a dollar about as easily as anybody else. And it's the same way about a lot of other things. We give ourselves credit for being long-headed and contriving, when the credit really ought to go to hard winters and high hills. Being snowed up for months at a stretch, year after year, was what really taught us to remember the three Yankee commandments and keep 'em holy. We——"

"Yankee what?" Jan laughed, but it was the way she'd laughed before.

"Commandments. They've got three extra ones, up there. Eat it up. Wear it out. Make it do. They don't set so much store by 'em nowadays, but there's plenty of old-timers that still swear by 'em, and plenty of places where they still have to live by 'em. Aunt Effie wouldn't have broken one of 'em any more than any of the other ten. I'd hear 'em every time I left scraps on my plate or wanted new pants instead of more patches on the old ones. Not because we were hard up. We weren't. There was a time when I wanted a baseball bat. I could have bought one for a quarter and I had the quarter, but Aunt Effie wasn't letting me break that Thirteenth Commandment. I could find something out in the barn and make it do."

"Did you?" Jan said.

"Oh, sure. I found an old wagon tongue and sawed the end off it and drawshaved it down. It worked all right. Better than any I could have bought for a quarter. It was the same way when I wanted a toboggan. I'd saved up the money to buy one, but the money stayed in the bank and I did my coasting on a sheet of old roofing-tin, with the front end of it curled up. I beat most of the boughten toboggans with it, at that."

"I wish I'd known your Aunt Effie," Jan said.

"You'd have liked her," Dusty said. "I'm making her sound stingy, but she wasn't. She was just doing her duty by me the way she saw it. No boy of hers was going to grow up with the idea that the only way to get things done was to hire somebody else to do 'em, and the only way to get things he wanted was to hiper down to a store and spend out hard money for 'em."

He laughed. Talking about Aunt Effie was making him talk like her. He'd almost forgotten that there was such a word as hiper. He could hear her saying it.

"I used to argue with her, but it never was any use. It wouldn't be her fault if I didn't learn good habits, and one of 'em was the habit of depending on myself and making shift do whatever I had to do with whatever I had to do it with. No matter where the argument started it would always end up with Lishe Bridger, and the time he went into the old jailhouse, over at Grimfield Center, to take shelter from a blizzard, and the door blew shut on him. Aunt Effie always wanted to know how much all good Lishe's money would have done him, locked in there with nobody liable to come within a mile of him for weeks or maybe months, if he hadn't been raised to do for himself, with whatever was handy. No way to get out but to cut a window-bar, and nothing to cut it with but his two hands and the yarn he unraveled out of a sock and some stone dust he scraped up off the floor, but——"

He stopped as the idea hit him.

"Go on," Jan said. "However could he cut through an iron bar with——?"

"Just the way we're going to—" Dusty was up on his feet, trying to keep his voice from shouting—"just the way we're going to saw off that casing and lick that fire!"

II

RICK'S HAND came away from his pocket with nothing in it. The dealer had shoved another stack halfway across the table. Rick shook his head at him.

"That'll be about all," he said. "Cash in, Stel. We're taking a powder."

Stella had been piking, as usual, and winning a little. The dealer gave her thirty dollars for her three stacks, and she tucked them carefully into her bag. There was nothing else in it. Stella didn't believe in carrying money unless she was carrying it home. Rick watched her shut the bag.

"You can blow me to a drink on the way out."

"I'll think about it," Stella said.

They went out to the front room. There was a line-up at the long bar but most of the little chromium tables were empty. They took the one in the corner. Rick ordered two Scotches. Stella shook her head.

"One. I can't seem to get any lift out of a drink when I'm paying for it myself."

It ought to have been good for a laugh, but it wasn't. Rick's face didn't change. Stella patted his arm.

"Come on, Rick. Be your age. What's it to you if Duss gives a girl a tumble? You've done it yourself a couple of times, unless somebody's been spreading scandal about you."

"Yeah. Only not like this. No dame I ever went for would have stood a chance of turning me sour on Duss, and none of 'em would have tried it over once. But this redhead's not only trying it, she's doing it. She's got him sold on that idea about me being a blanket Osage with a yen for gold spittoons. She's filled him up with eyewash till he's all set to walk out on me. Till he wants to quit a racket where he's absolute, all-time tops and start in trying to outsmart birds like Dan Rogan at their own game! And she isn't doing it because she's got any use for Duss—she hasn't any. She's doing it because she hates my guts and this is her way to louse me up! And all I can do about it is to keep right on trying to lick her fire for her!"

He drank half his Scotch.

"And when I lick it, what happens? We own a piece of a lease, and Duss gives me the air so he can go in business and be respectable, like Dan Rogan!"

Stella didn't say anything. Her eyes were narrowed a little and she made wet circles on the table with the bottom of the soda-bottle. She was still doing it when Jim Hafey came in. He started for the bar and then stopped and came over to the table.

Rick deadpanned him, but Hafey didn't seem to feel any chill in the air. He spread himself over a chair and mopped his face.

"I've been looking for you," he said.

"Yeah," Rick said. "I heard the bloodhounds."

"All right." Hafey chuckled. "I did have a hunch you might be here. I've got a proposition that might interest you if you feel like talking business for a minute."

"I'll listen that long," Rick said.

"That'll be enough." Hafey mopped his chops again. "You and Miller own ten thousand shares of M-H stock. I'll give you a dollar a share for it."

"You wouldn't want to put in a bid on the Brooklyn Bridge, would you?" Rick said.

"I mean it." Hafey reached into the bulge of his seersucker jacket and showed the edges of sheafed new bills.

"I can hear you better, now," Rick said. "Shoot."

"I'll face 'em for you. The way things are going Jan and I'll be owing somebody a nice large piece of money by the time that fire's licked. That wouldn't worry me. But we'll be owing it to World Pete, and that worries me plenty."

"You're getting timid," Rick said.

"And how! But Jan isn't. Rogan's wearing white wings in her book, and every time he gets us deeper in the hole they look whiter to her. Maybe she doesn't need to worry. Rogan might be figuring on marrying her. But he ain't figuring on marrying me.

I know where I'll be sitting when he puts the squeeze on us."

"You said something about ten grand," Rick said. "Use up the rest of your minute talking about that."

"I still got some friends and some of 'em ain't flat," Hafey said. "I raised this ten and I can get more where it came from. Enough more to square up what we owe World Pete now and to keep after the fire. But I can't do it without control of the company. Otherwise I'm deadlocked with a muleheaded kid who won't hear to reason. That's the picture. You got my top offer. And talking about minutes, I'll give you yours back. You got that long to take it or leave it."

Stella had kept on making circles with the bottom of the bottle. She stopped, now, and looked up.

"Leave it, Rick," she said.

Rick's mouth pulled flat.

"I'm handling this." He turned to Hafey. "I'll make you another proposition," he said slowly. "If I sell you this stock we'll still owe you a licked fire, according to the deal I made with the redhead. Call that off and it's a bet. You pay us ten grand for the work we've done this far and I hand you back the wallpaper. Okay?"

Hafey took a little while to think. Then he nodded. He pulled the money out of his pocket and pushed it across the table. Rick brought out his wallet and fished the stock certificate out of it. Hafey took it and stood up. All at once he seemed to remember about being old and fat and tired.

"See you in church," he said. He slouched over to the door and went out. Stella's glance followed him.

"It's kind of funny, his digging up this much sudden money," she said.

"It's a hell of a lot funnier, my getting my hooks on it, right when I'm down to where I'd be hanging my cigarettes on somebody's cuff!" Rick laughed. "And it's funnier yet to get it without having to even give the redhead's fire a dirty look! And the biggest laugh of all is having Duss where he can't even kid himself he's in the oil business!"

"I was thinking about that," Stella said. "That's why I tried to stop you. Duss isn't going to like it."

"What kick has he got?" Rick's face froze up again. "I get us ten grand for a job we don't even have to finish. A job we might be working on till we get long white whiskers. I fix it so we're loose to go after the real dough down at Bayou Rouge any time we want it. Come on. Let's go back and take another crack at those dice before they find out this is my lucky night."

Stella reached out for the money. She handled it like a bank-teller, splitting it into two neat piles. She put one of the piles into her bag. Rick scowled.

"What's the idea?"

"Nothing," Stella said. "Only when you start telling Dusty all about this big favor you've been doing him, it might go over better if his half of the money is in my bag instead of Mink Schwartz's safe."

Rick looked ugly for a second. Then he laughed.

"Okay, baby. Have it your way. But don't waste any worry over Duss ever getting sore at anything I do. He wouldn't know how."

"You ought to know," Stella said. "You've tried about every way there is." She fingered the bills in her bag. "I wish I didn't feel as if there was something funny about this money. I keep wondering where Jim Hafey could have got it."

12

Jim Hafey drove slowly out Carondelet Street. At the corner of Bossuet he drew in to the curb and stopped. Dan Rogan's voice came quietly out of a blot of black shadow under a magnolia, but Rogan himself stayed where he was.

"Nice work, Hafey."

"Yeah," Hafey said. "Damn nice."

"Now what's the matter?" Rogan's voice sharpened a little. "You got it, didn't you?"

"Sure I got it." Hafey leaned out and handed over the certificate. Rogan chuckled.

"I thought you would. It's a wonder that Farren's held onto it this long!" His voice cooled and hardened. "Why didn't you tell me he had it? If I'd known that——"

"I didn't know it myself till you told me," Hafey said. "What's the difference? You've got it, now. You can put the freeze on Frank Morel any time you want to."

"You don't seem to fancy the idea." Rogan laughed again. "You wouldn't be developing a conscience, would you, at your time of life?"

"Conscience, hell!" Hafey said. "Lay off me, Rogan. I got to help you take Frank Morel's kid to the cleaners, but I don't have to like it, and I don't. You're welcome to all the kick you can get out of this one."

"Use sense." Rogan's voice was icy. "You know that whoever may be taken to the cleaners, as you put it, it won't be Miss Morel. What has happened merely puts you in a position to sell control of your company to World Petroleum. If you decide to do so——"

"If!" Hafey laughed heavily.

"Very well, then. When. When you decide to do so, you will of course insist on my buying Morel's stock along with your own, and at the same price." Rogan paused. "The same price. And I think you mean to see that it is a fairly high price, don't you?"

Hafey whistled, a long, low note.

"Like that, huh? You're part human, after all! You're figuring on marrying her!"

"I think we won't discuss that," Rogan said.

"Okay," Hafey said. "I'd sooner talk about something else, myself."

"All right. We'll talk about your own M-H stock. It's still in hock, I suppose, at the Petra bank?"

"You know it is," Hafey said. "So what?"

"You'd better pay off the loan tomorrow," Rogan said. "I have the cash here for you. You can mail the stock to me. I'll feel a little safer about it when it's in my own hands." He snickered softly. "Not that I don't trust you, of course."

He handed over a fat envelope. Hafey took it and, without answering Rogan's curt, dismissing good night, drove back to the Beauregard-McGee.

Dusty Miller was in the lobby. Hafey stopped at

the sight of him and turned, but not quickly enough. Dusty came running after him.

"I got it, Jim!" He clapped a hand on Hafey's shoulder. "We've got that fire licked right now! All we need to do is——"

"Save it," Hafey said. "You ain't even interested in that fire. You're all through."

Dusty stared. Then he laughed.

"You had me going, for a second. I thought you meant it."

"Don't kid yourself I didn't," Hafey said. "It goes. I had a talk with Rick, tonight, and settled up with him. You're calling it a day, and so am I."

"I don't get you," Dusty said. "I tell you I can——"

Hafey waddled over to a chair and lowered himself into it.

"Sit down, kid. I been over all this with your partner, but I guess I got to spell it out again for you. It's like this."

He had the story pat, by now. He made it sound even better than when he had told it to Rick.

"It was no use talking to Jan. I guess you know

how much chance anybody'd stand of changing her mind about Rogan. So I went at it the other way. I dug me up a piece of money and bought me back the ten thousand shares that Rick and you——"

"You what?" Dusty started to stand up. Hafey waved him back down again.

"Keep your shirt on, kid. You're out of it pretty. The deal was that you had to lick the fire before you owned them shares, and the way things were going, they wouldn't have been worth a damn a dozen even with the fire out. This way you don't need to lick it and you go south with ten thousand fish. You got no squawk coming."

Dusty had hold of himself by now. He mustn't start thinking about Rick. Not yet.

"Look," he said. "This doesn't change things any, except that you own a bigger piece of the fire than you did before. You've got just that much more reason for wanting it licked, and I can lick it for you. I'll do it on the same deal as before. I'll——"

"Not for me you won't," Hafey said. He sounded as tired as he looked. "Whoever douses this one will be doing it for somebody else. I know where I can sell the lease, fire and all, for enough to last me out my time, and I'm doing it while I still got something to sell. I might get more, playing it your way, and I might get nothing. I'm playing it my way."

"How about Jan?" Dusty said. "You're selling her out, too."

"And I'm getting her plenty. More'n she'd ever have got if I'd laid back and left her keep on going in debt to Dan Rogan." Hafey stood up, wearily. "I'm sorry, kid. Maybe you could lick this fire and maybe not, but I've got to where I'm not making any more blind bets. If you got the answer, you can make your deal with whoever buys me out. All I know is you can't make it with me. I'm through. G'night, kid."

Dusty watched him shuffle over toward the elevators. After a while he went up to the suite and started packing his bags. He quit, though, before he finished. His mind was wide awake but his body was all in. It was so tired that even his mind gave up, pretty soon, and went to sleep.

He woke up early and finished packing. He called the desk and had them send up for his bags. The boys were just carrying them out into the hall when Rick and Stella got out of the elevator. Except for the sooty smudges under her eyes, Stella looked as if she'd just stepped out of a beauty parlor. Rick was weaving a little, but that was all. He steadied himself with a hand against the door frame.

"What's the big idea, Duss?" He tried a laugh but it didn't quite come off. "Don't we live here any more?"

"We don't live anywhere any more," Dusty said. He bore down a little on the "we". Rick nodded.

"So that's how you feel, huh?"

"What do you think?" Dusty said.

"Okay." Rick's mouth hardly moved. "Have it your way."

"It's your way," Dusty said. "You fixed it this way when you framed this play. You washed us all up when you sold that stock. You knew we didn't own it. You talked Jan into trusting us with it and when you double-crossed her you made crooks out of both of us. You——"

"Listen, Duss," Stella cut in, "Rick never——"

"Skip it, Stella," Dusty said. "You ought to be

satisfied. You're getting your wish. You've been trying to split the team ever since——"

"Not like this," Stella said. "Rick was only——"

"I know," Dusty said. "Only trying to keep me tied into his racket. So all he does is louse me out of what might be my chance to quit."

"So you finally got me figured out, huh?" Rick didn't move a muscle in his face and his voice stayed on one flat tone. "Looks like I must've put on a good act, keeping you fooled all this while."

Dusty shook his head.

"No. You weren't putting on any act and you didn't have me fooled. That's what's washing us up. Not what you did to me, last night, nor even what you did to Jan. What you did to Rick Farren. To the right guy I used to be teamed up with. Up to last night he was aces, every way there was. And last night you rubbed him out. You turned him into a——"

He stopped, but not to hunt for the word he wanted. He had that picked out. He stopped because he wanted it to hit hard.

"—into a heel."

He didn't look back, going down the hall to the elevator. Rick stood very still, watching him, one hand behind him, steadying him by the door frame. His face stayed frozen. Stella took a slow look at it. Then she opened her bag and started fumbling in it.

"Well, we got one break. He forgot all about his half of the money."

"And that's a break, huh?" Rick's eyes were black marbles. "I see. I'm a heel by you, too, huh? I just go south with Duss's dough, do I?"

Stella shook her head. "You go dig up Jim Hafey and buy that stock back. I tried to stop you from selling it but I could see it wasn't any use. The only way for you to find how it was going to make you look to Dusty was to let him tell you. And now he's told you, we show him he's wrong. We buy back the stock and——"

Rick's head jerked up. For a second his face came alive, but only for a second.

"You're okay, Stel. But it's no dice. Where would I raise the other five grand, even if——"

"Ask me a hard one," Stella said. She went by him

into the sitting room of the suite and motioned for him to shut the door. "Where does anybody get money? You just borrow it from the bank, of course!"

"Yeah?" Rick said. "What bank?"

"The First National, unconscious." Her hand reached under her skirt and brought out a flat silk purse, shaped like an envelope. She pried a tight lump of bills out of it, folded twice. She unfolded them and peeled off five. She wadded the others into the purse again and put it back where it had come from.

Rick's jaw was sagging.

"Where'd you get this?"

"Oh, be your age! You've been watching me get it. What did you think I was doing with my cut from Mink Schwartz and my kickbacks from Guldenberg and all the rest of it? You throw it around and I pick some of it up and keep it for you, and now you need it, you've got it."

Rick fingered the bills a minute and then pushed them back to her.

"You want to watch your step, Stel. The first thing

you know you'll have me changing my ideas about you. Keep your dough, though. Hafey needed that stock a whole lot more than he needed his ten grand. He won't be handing it back for what he paid."

"Want to bet?" Stella said. She went over to the telephone. "Is Mr. Hafey registered? No. Don't ring him. Just give me the room number and I'll call him later. Thanks."

She hung up.

"Come on. And don't be in too much of a hurry about changing your ideas about me. You might have to change 'em back."

They rode down to the twelfth floor. Stella tapped on the door with the tips of her fingernails. That was a trick of hers. It was hardly loud enough for Rick to hear it but she only had to tap twice to make Hafey hear it. His voice, thick and blurry with sleep, came through the door.

"Who is it?"

"It's me. Stella Conway." Stella said it quietly. "It's about Dan Rogan, Jim. You'd better let me in —quick."

The latch clicked and Hafey's face, bleary-eyed,

showed at the edge of the door. He tried to shut it when he saw Rick but Stella was in the way. She pushed in and Rick followed her.

"What's the idea?" Hafey was in baggy pajamas. His white hair was tousled.

"Rick's brought you back your money, Jim. He's changed his mind about selling you that stock. I told him you'd be glad to let him have it back, if I asked you to."

Hafey stared at her, slackjawed.

"I hope you know what you're driving at," he said.

"Maybe I do," Stella said. "Maybe I even know a few more things. I knew a pretty good way to get that door open in a hurry, didn't I?"

Hafey shook his head as if he was trying to shake the sleep out of it.

"Listen, Jim," Stella said. "I know you're working for Rogan. I've known it ever since the night I sat outside of the phone booth at Mink Schwartz's and heard you get the news from him that your wildcat was on fire. That started me remembering things."

"What things?" Hafey's face was a giveaway, but he tried to bluster.

"Well, for instance, I remembered that in spite of all the hymn of hate you're always singing about Rogan you do quite a lot of business with World Pete through him. He handled the deal when they bought your Rodessa leases, for instance, and they paid you plenty. But in a month you were flat again and nobody saw you spend a dime for anything but rum. I got to wondering whether maybe it hadn't been Rogan's money you used to pay for those leases and if it wasn't Rogan who got most of the profit when you sold them. Of course that's only a guess, but there's one thing I'm not guessing about."

She waited but Hafey didn't say anything.

"I don't have to guess about what kind of a guy you are, Jim. I know. It wouldn't worry you any to help Rogan chisel a million out of World Pete—not if you got a piece of it. But nobody can tell me that you'd help Rogan rob as good a friend of yours as Frank Morel. The only reason you could be helping Rogan rawdeal Morel and his kid would be that you couldn't help yourself. That isn't any guess, Jim. Not for anybody that knows you. And it can't mean but one thing. Rogan's got a whip over you and he's cracking it. He's got something on you that——"

"Go ahead," Hafey said. "Get the whole of your pipe-dream off your mind, now you've started. Only if you think you can shake me down with it——"

"I'm not trying to shake you down," Stella said. "I'm just asking you to sell Rick back that stock as a kind of favor to me. And I'm offering to do you a favor if you will. A big one."

"You sound like it!" Hafey grunted.

"I am, though. Let's suppose I've got the right idea. Let's suppose that you hate helping Rogan work this squeeze on the Morel girl, and the only reason you're doing it is because you have to take orders from Rogan, no matter what they are. I'd be doing you a favor, wouldn't I, if I showed you how you could quit taking orders from him?"

Hafey's head lifted quickly. He didn't speak, though.

"Let's suppose he's got something on you. Let's suppose he's got enough to send you to the chair. How is he going to use it? What's going to happen to him and his juicy job with World Pete when you start telling the world about that Rodessa deal, and a few more like it? And what's going to stop you from talking, when you've got nothing left to lose?"

Hafey's face came to life, slowly, like a man waking out of a bad dream.

He let out a laugh, a short sharp one, like a dog's yelp.

"And I never thought of it! Letting that fish-faced bastard crack his whip over me for six years and never asking myself what'd happen to him if he went to hit me with it! I'll say you done me a favor, Stel! Rogan's got your stock. Go ask him for it—the way you been asking me! I'm betting you don't have to ask him over once!"

"I don't believe I will, either," Stella said. "Not after you've dealt me a few more cards. All I've got now is three guesses and a pair of hopes and some way I don't feel they'd be enough to steal the pot from Dan Rogan."

"Don't worry," Hafey said. "You're gonna have four aces and the joker!"

"Nothing stirring," Rick said. His voice was sharp-edged. Stella's head turned toward him, her eyebrows arched.

"You don't take a chance on any play like that," Rick said. "You'd be safer trying to bluff a rattler! Rogan might back down but he'd remember. You're keeping out, all the way!"

Stella's eyebrows stayed up.

"Hafey gets the stock back from Rogan," Rick said. "Rogan'll know he isn't bluffing."

Stella shook her head slowly.

"That won't work," she said. There was a different sound in her voice that matched the difference in her face. "Jim doesn't have to be afraid of Rogan, but neither does Rogan have to be afraid of Jim. They've both got whips, all right, but neither of them can use them."

"That's right." Rick's eyebrows pulled together. He kept them that way for a minute. Then he laughed.

"It works," he said. "Look, Hafey. You just go tell Rogan that I changed my mind about selling you that stock and want to buy it back. That'll be a laugh to him, till you go on and break the news to him that I know all about whatever it is he's got on you, and if you don't hand me back the stock I start talking.

See? If he hangs onto the stock and you go over the hill to the Big Stone House, what have you got to lose by spilling all you know about him? And will you do it or will you just do it?"

Hafey thought it over. Then he laughed, a wheezy chuckle, and held out a fat, brick-red hand.

13

ALTHOUGH few unwelcome visitors ever gained admission to Dan Rogan's inner office, Jim Hafey, very manifestly not welcome, had gained entry without difficulty or delay.

"Well?" Rogan's face and voice had both been in the icebox. "I thought I told you——"

"Save it," Hafey said. Unasked, he helped himself to a chair. He mopped his chops. "Hell's loose, Rogan, and no pitch hot. Farren wants his stock back, and I've got to give it to him."

"I still don't see why you felt it necessary to come here in person, instead of using the telephone."

"Listen, Rogan, forget about being a bigshot for a minute. You can climb back upon your high chair when I'm gone. I didn't phone you because you couldn't hand me the stock over the wire and I need it right away, this very now. If Farren doesn't get it by ten o'clock——"

"He doesn't get it, then or later," Rogan said.

"Guess again," Hafey said. "He knows all about that—that mixup down at Santone."

Rogan sat perfectly still for a little while. Then his mouth unbuttoned itself into a thin smile.

"That's unfortunate for you, Hafey. But I fail to see why you should imagine that it involves me."

"Take another look," Hafey said. "Try and see me, chopping cotton on the State Farm, knowing what I know and keeping it all under my hat. After all you've been doing for me, I wouldn't want to make any trouble for you, would I?"

Rogan's mouth buttoned itself up again.

"I'd certainly keep quiet about these jobs I been doing for you, wouldn't I, if I didn't have anything to lose by talking?" Hafey said. "And could I prove who I been doing 'em for! You were so damn sure I couldn't ever afford to use what I had on you that you didn't care how much I got. And did I get plenty!"

Rogan's fingers tapped gently on the glass top of his desk.

"Yes," he said. "As far as you're concerned, Hafey, I'm afraid I've been a little negligent. I ought to have foreseen this possibility and I didn't." He stopped. "You're quite sure that Farren really knows——?"

"He knows, all right," Hafey said.

"And you think he'll talk unless he gets the stock?"

"If you think he's bluffing, you're free to call him," Hafey said. "I wouldn't, but if you want to take the chance, have 'em send him in here. He and Stella Conway are waiting for me out front."

Rogan sat up straighter.

"You brought them here?"

"Yeah," Hafey said. "Just like the rabbit brought home the hound dog. Never mind the squawk, Rogan. Those two were sticking right to me till they got that stock. The best I could do was to get in here without 'em."

"How much do they know?" Rogan said. "About me, I mean?"

"They know you got the stock," Hafey said.

"Yes, and how much else?"

"That's all I told 'em," Hafey said.

Rogan tapped on the desk again.

"Let's see. This has to be handled so that I don't seem to be acting under pressure. I'll have to have a reason for surrendering the stock or——" Rogan touched the switch of the communicator. "Send in Miss Conway and Mr. Farren." He turned to Hafey. "Keep out of it. I'll do the talking." He stood up as Stella and Rick came in. He motioned them toward chairs in the manner of a condescending dictator.

"Good morning, Stella. Good morning, Farren. This interview will have to be brief, so that I am stating my position at once and finally. Hafey tells me that unless he is able to resell you, at the price he paid for it, some M-H stock which he subsequently sold to me, he will be in serious trouble. Frankly, that would incline me to refuse. I don't like Hafey and I wouldn't lift a finger to oblige him. I bought the stock simply to protect Miss Morel's interests and I——"

"Come on. Get brief yourself, Rogan," Rick said. "You don't have to tell me what a swell guy you are. I know. Do I get the stock?"

"Be nice, Rick," Stella said. "Dan's a business-man. He's got something you want and there's no reason why he should let go of it just to oblige you. He's just working up to a proposition, aren't you, Dan?"

Rogan gave her the icebox smile.

"Thank you, Stella. You're quite right. And here is the proposition, Farren. I'll sell you back the stock at what I paid if you'll undertake to handle the Bayou Rouge fire for me at my original figure of fifteen thousand. Take it or leave it. I haven't time for any bargaining."

Rick glanced at Stella. She nodded.

"It's a bet." Rick put the money on the desk. "Where's the stock?"

Rogan took the certificate out of his pocket. He hesitated a moment and handed it over. A short, explosive sound, like a snort, escaped from Hafey.

Rogan's eyes slanted at him inquiringly, but Hafey was looking at Stella, and his expression drew Rogan's glance to her. He frowned a little. There didn't seem to be any valid reason why Hafey should be eyeing with unmistakable approval, almost with affection, a very tired woman, with black smudges under her eyes, who was rather boredly repainting with purple lipstick a wide, droop-cornered mouth.

Rogan did not ask Hafey about it, though, when they were again alone. There was something more important to be discovered.

"How about your stock, Hafey?"

"It's right here." Hafey tapped his pocket. "I stopped in at the bank on the way over and paid up the loan."

"Well, hand it over." Rogan spoke impatiently. "What are you waiting for?"

Hafey looked him over almost compassionately.

"For hell to freeze over, Rogan," he said. "If that isn't soon enough for you, maybe you can think up something you can do about it."

He was whistling as he went over toward the door, and there was hardly any sag in his shoulders.

14

"I JUST can't believe it of Jim Hafey," Jan said. "It's bad enough for me, but it's going to be just awful for Dad. He's always sworn by Jim. He wouldn't even try to get anybody else to drill for us. Jim's going back on us will be harder for Dad to take than losing the lease." She looked around her quickly at the long, bare, friendly room. "Even harder than losing the place."

"It won't be that bad," Dusty said. "Hafey won't sell without taking care of you. He—it's funny, but I couldn't seem to get very sore at him. He's got some excuse, I mean. He's old and tired and licked. But I know how it makes you feel. All the rest of it would be easy to take, compared to having Rick turn out to be a heel."

"I know," Jan said. "But as long as he is one, it's better for you to know it now. You're through with him and you're through with his crazy business, too."

"I was through with that, anyway," Dusty said. "This was going to be my last job." He stopped. Losing Rick was still the worst of it, but he was losing plenty besides. He hadn't realized, until it was lost, how much it was and how much he'd been wanting it. He hadn't quite admitted to himself that when he thought about owning oil wells, drilling new ones, about making a real life for himself, with real work to do, with peace and comfort and quiet contentment waiting for him at the day's end, all he'd really been thinking about had been Jan Morel. Maybe that had always been a laugh. It was a laugh now, anyway.

"And talking about jobs reminds me I'll be needing one. And a swell chance I'll stand of getting it!"

"Don't be foolish," Jan said. "That's one thing you don't have to worry about. You can have any kind of a job you want. Everybody in the business knows you."

"Everybody in the business knows I can fight fires. That'll be a big help getting me a job at anything else!" He laughed. "It'll be a big help, too, the kind of a rep Rick and I've been hanging on ourselves. A couple of lunatics. Taking a job when we got good and ready, holding out for the last dime there was in it and then kicking the gong around till we were flat again! Sure. Any business-man would trip over his own feet trying to pin me on the payroll!"

"I know one who'd do just that," Jan said. "Dan Rogan."

"If anything could give me a laugh right now that would hand me a swell one," Dusty said.

"I mean it. He was talking about you yesterday, out at the lease. He isn't classing you with Rick. Not for a minute. He kept telling me I didn't need to worry about the fire. He said I could bet on you to finish any job you tackled."

"I could finish that one, anyhow," Dusty said. He didn't want to go on talking about Rogan. He didn't want to think about him. Rogan would be having things all his own way, now, with Jan. The growly feeling came into Dusty's throat. It was better to think about something else, anything else, than what was going to happen to Jan if she kept on believing in Rogan. "Let's make another try at locating Hafey. If I could just get to him and make him listen——"

The old doorbell tinkled quietly. Zenie shuffled past the doorway, her carpet-slippers slithering on the bare floor. Dusty came up on his feet as Rick walked in. It didn't seem possible that only yesterday he would have been glad to see that deadpan face.

"Get out," he said.

"No, Duss." Jan's voice was eager. "Don't——"

"Get out," Dusty said again.

"Sure," Rick said. "I only stopped in to give you your wallpaper."

He flipped the certificate on the table and started for the doorway. It was Jan who got around in front of him. Dusty couldn't have moved.

"Wait, Rick," Jan said. "You've got to tell us what happened. How did you ever get Jim to give it back?"

"Jim didn't have it, Red." Rick looked over her

head at Dusty. "He'd sold it before I got to him. But you got a break there. The guy he sold it to turned out to be a buddy of yours by the name of Rogan."

"Dan?" Jan sounded as if she didn't quite believe it.

"Sure," Rick said. He kept on looking at Dusty. "But he was only trying to protect you. He said so himself. He was afraid Hafey might sell out to somebody who wouldn't be so friendly to you. As soon as I told him I wanted it for Duss he was glad to sell it back."

"Oh, I see," Jan said. "For a minute I thought——"

The telephone buzzed and she went over to it. Rick moved closer to Dusty.

"Listen, Duss. I know I looked kind of bad, but——"

"How do I look?" Dusty said. "Thinking you were——"

"Forget it," Rick said. "You had a right to think plenty. You had a right to slap me down—if you'd had your army along. I was ginned up and sore and didn't see what a dirty deal I was handing you."

"Wash it out," Dusty said. "How did you pry the stock out of Rogan?"

"Oh, there was nothing to that," Rick said. "Stella just asked him for it."

He waited for Dusty to get through laughing.

"And now we got our nice wallpaper back, how about going out there and earning it," he said. "Hafey was telling me you had an idea."

"It's in the bag," Dusty said. "All we need is about six hundred feet of light wireline and some valve-grinding paste, and—" he grinned, "and a damn fool to go in close enough to get a loop over the casing."

Rick thought it over for a minute.

"You might have something there," he said. "You ask dear old Dan Rogan for a little more World Pete wireline and dig up your valve stuff somewhere and we're all set. We already got the damn fool."

Jan had finished telephoning. Dusty twisted his eyes away from her.

"Maybe we've got two of those," he said.

15

THEY had planted a section of casing so that it stood about the right height above the ground, and Rick was trying to throw a loop of wireline over it. He had got so he didn't miss more than three times out of four, but the loop wasn't very long. Nowhere near long enough, Dusty thought, glancing over his shoulder toward the fire. And it was going to be more of a trick, in there. He pushed Rick away from the line.

"You need more body swing in it," he shouted. "Like throwing the hammer. This way."

He stopped and took hold of the doubled line,

swung the loop behind him and then shot it ahead and up. It ringed the casing. He pulled the line back and made a new loop, longer this time. It ringed the casing, too. But when Rick tried it he hardly got the loop off the ground. He kept on trying and he kept on getting worse as his temper tightened him up.

"Let me take a shot at it," Dusty said. He lengthened out the loop a little further, swung and missed, swung again and caught the casing. Rick pushed him out of the way as he was starting for another try.

"One side." His voice was ugly. "You're only wasting time. You can make me look bad, sure, and what does that get us? I'm the one that's got to do the trick when we're in there."

Dusty shook his head. The idea had hit him between the eyes.

"Guess again," he said. "When we're in there you'll be handling the hose." Rick stared at him.

"I can loop that casing from farther off than you can and that's that," Dusty said. "If it was only an inch difference we still couldn't afford to give it away."

"Yeah," Rick said. His voice wasn't so ugly, now,

but it was just as stubborn. "Only the difference might be the other way, in there. I been in oftener than you have and further. That might make up for me not being so hot at throwing the hammer."

Dusty could see he'd have to find another argument. He thought fast.

"Look, Rick. We finally found one thing about this business I can do as well as you can, and I ought to get my crack at it. You've been out in the limelight plenty of times. You could afford to give me this one shot at it."

Rick's face thawed out a little, but he kept on shaking his head.

"That limelight's plenty warm, kid. You wouldn't like it."

Dusty could see it was no use, but he had to keep on trying. Rick would never get the loop where it had to go, but telling him so would only make him more muleheaded about it. The only thing that might work was to keep on pretending to want the spotlight. Dusty was just going to try that again when he saw the Pierce coming along the plank road and forgot all about Rick, till he heard him chuckle.

"Okay, Romeo. I get it, now. Here comes your grandstand. Go out there in the box and pitch."

Dusty's mind came back to business with a jerk.

"Let's go," he said. He started for the shack. All he had to do, now, was to be on his way before Jan got here and made it any harder for him to be walking away from her.

He didn't quite manage that. He and Rick were just getting helped into their asbestos suits when she came past the corner of the shack. She'd been hurrying, Dusty saw. He didn't know whether he was glad about that or sorry.

"Just in time, Red," Rick said. "You pretty near missed the show, and you'd sure have been missing something! We changed the act. I'm handling the hose on this one and Duss is gonna be the daring young man on the flying trapeze."

Jan had started a smile. It didn't get very far. Dusty wasn't quite quick enough about looking as if Rick was only joking.

"Not really?" Her voice had a sort of tightness in it. "You aren't going to do it, are you, Duss?"

"You ought to know Rick by now," Dusty said. It

was a queer feeling, not wanting her to worry and wanting her to, both at once. "Come on, Rick. Let's go."

He turned to let Guthead help him on with the helmet. He knew that if he didn't get away in a hurry it was going to be worse, and it was bad enough. No matter how stupid it was to feel that way, Jan's being here, looking the way she looked, made him want to stay alive harder than he'd ever wanted to before. He waved to her as he and Rick started away. Her hand moved a little, as if it was trying to wave back and couldn't, and somehow that was better than if it had waved.

The new wireline was ready, the middle section loaded with the valve-compound. The crew had pulled it up pretty close to the fire, but there was plenty of distance left. With Guthead and Ivan Gary handling the hoses, Rick and Dusty worked a loop of it further in, pushing the shield ahead of them into the narrowing, shifting cave in the fire, where the broken valve shot the flame off to each side. They dropped the loop and came back, pulling the shield after them, and got a new grip on the doubled line, farther back, and dragged the doubled loop in almost as far as they had taken the single one. Dusty got a kick out of the strength it cost to make that second trip; if he hadn't figured this stunt out he'd be trying to drag this much weight and more, all by himself, for the last few steps, when he'd need to be making speed and saving strength. This way he'd only have a short loop to haul.

They went back again. Rick got behind another shield and took hold of the light hose. It was in a zigzag, so it wouldn't be any harder for him to haul than it had to be. Dusty had thought that one up, too. The streams from the two heavier hoses could reach all the way into the middle of the fire but the men who handled them couldn't always see that far. Rick would be in close enough to keep his light hose on Dusty, even if the wind shifted the fire so that the men outside lost sight of him.

Dusty went ahead, alone this time. He'd been expecting to be scared, but he wasn't. There wasn't time enough, and there was too much else to do. He seemed to have turned off the lights inside of his mind except the ones he needed for the job. He wasn't thinking about anything, now, except the distance to that whitehot mass of steel ahead of him and the length of the wireline loop he was dragging behind him. Almost far enough . . . another step, and another . . . this was it. He turned, ducked through the stream from Rick's hose, got his grip on the line. Like throwing the hammer. The same trick of giving it everything you had, all at once . . . he had a glimpse of the snaking loop as it swung out and rose. Even before his hands had quite let go he knew they hadn't missed.

Back, now, pulling the shield, into the smash of Rick's hose . . . into the heavier smash of the bigger ones . . . no helmet, any more . . . air coming deep down into him and not hurting . . . Rick's voice, sliding through the snarl of the fire, calling him cowboy. . . . And Jan.

"You—you heel, Duss! You——" He could barely hear her voice, but he could hear it well enough not to mind about its calling him a heel. "You liar!" He didn't mind that, either. He'd never mind anything, he guessed, that Jan said to him, as long as she looked at him the way she was looking at him now, with tears running down across the little bridge of freckles. It didn't matter what she called him, as long as she used that voice to do it with, as long as her arms were tight about his neck and her mouth was almost touching his. No. Not almost, now. . . .

Her hands kept hold of him when she pulled away a little.

"Damn you!" she said. "If you ever do that to me again, I'll——" She stopped. "Are you all right? Are you——?"

Dusty nodded, laughing. There was something comical about the idea that anything, ever, could be anything except all right. It was even all right for Rick to be standing beside him, using the saw-tooth voice on Jan.

"Look, Red. Can't you read? Don't you see the sign says 'Men at Work'?"

"I don't care what the sign says," Jan said. "Duss isn't going back in there!"

"Don't worry," Rick said. "Nobody's going in there. Not even me. But that don't mean there's nothing left for Duss to do except play Barrymore. I've seen fires licked plenty of other ways but I never noticed any getting kissed to death."

"Have your fun," Dusty said. He wasn't sore, in

spite of what he knew was back of Rick's look and voice. "I'll be back to earth in a minute. You wouldn't want to help, would you, by giving me a hand?"

He held out the big asbestos mitt. After a second Rick reached out and touched it, but his face didn't change. Dusty didn't blame him taking it hard. Feeling the way he did about all women, Rick was bound to hate seeing any friend of his falling for one.

"It's all right, Jan. From here in we're coasting."

"Yes. And before you went in there you said——"

"That was a long time ago," Dusty said. "And things were different."

He watched the change in her face and knew that she understood, that she was finding out, as he had suddenly found it out, that there couldn't be any talk between them, after this, except straight talk. The truth, all of it, nothing else. That was how it had to be.

She gave him a little nod and moved her hand. He and Rick went over to where the crew were making the ends of the looped wireline fast to the drawbars of two of World Pete's Diesel caterpillars. With the loop all the way around the casing the caterpillars shuttled back and forth, drawing the taut line between them. Dusty watched a while and came back to Jan.

"Nothing to it now but waiting," he said. "We can do that where it's cooler."

They went back beyond the worst of the hotness and climbed up onto a World Pete truck. With the fire filling the world with sound and fury talking meant shouting and the things Dusty wanted to say weren't things to be shouted. Jan seemed to feel the same way. Except for what her smile kept telling him, and her eyes, she didn't talk about anything except the fire and this plan of his for putting it out. She didn't understand that yet; he'd told her what it was but there hadn't been time to explain it.

"It's the same way Lishe Bridger cut his way out of the jail, only all he had to work with was yarn and stonedust. He'd take a piece of yarn, work some wet stonedust into it, take a turn around the bar and saw back and forth till the yarn wore out. Then he'd take a fresh piece and do it again. He just about starved and froze before he got his cut deep enough for him to break what was left of the bar. It won't take us so long. That wireline is loaded with something better than stonedust and it won't wear out, either. All we've got to do is keep those two caterpillars hauling it back and forth till it chews through the casing. The only tough part of the job's back of us—getting a loop of the line around the casing. There's a lot of wrecked concrete foundation in there, or we wouldn't have needed to go in with the line. If it hadn't been for the concrete being in the way we could have just anchored one end of the line and carried the other one around, outside of the fire. As it was, the only thing to do was to go in and lasso the casing, like a cowpunch throwing a rope. Rick couldn't throw it far enough, when he tried it out here, so I had to trade places with him."

He wanted to let it go at that, but he couldn't. The truth, all of it.

"I'd have had to do it anyway, though. This wasn't Rick's job. He wouldn't have been in there at all if it hadn't been for me."

He watched her face. He didn't know much about women but he knew there were lots of things they didn't see the way men saw them. It would be all right if Jan didn't understand why he had to be out in front on this job, but if she did understand it—he felt his breath go down deeper as her face told him that she did.

They waited a long time, watching the tractors shuttle back and forth, but it didn't seem long. It might have been minutes instead of hours afterwards that the fire suddenly changed into a tall, straight plume of flame and the screaming snarl of it deepened to a roar.

Dusty started climbing down. Jan caught his arm.

"You don't go back there!"

He met her eyes squarely.

"I just let Rick do it for me? For us?"

He was holding his breath again, watching the conflict in her face, but he knew, this time, how it would end.

"No. You have to go. But never again! I've got to know this is the last time. Promise?"

Dusty made the cross-mark over his heart.

"The last time. And it's nothing to worry about. Honestly. Rick and I could do the rest of it in our sleep. Chin up?"

She lifted it.

The long pipe they were going to use for a capping-manifold was ready, swung from the boom of the big caterpillar crane. Dusty didn't seem to mind walking out toward the fire, this time. He knew how Rick felt about fires, now. They weren't anything. You just went up to them and slapped them down.

That was what he and Rick did to this one. The manifold came down over the clean-cut casing; the fire shot from the top of it, high overhead.

That was all. The crew could finish the job now. Rick turned and started for the shack. Dusty went after him. This was one time when licking a fire didn't seem to key Rick up. He had on his deadpan face and he kept it on while he and Dusty hosed each other down and dressed, and he didn't answer when Dusty tried to talk. He didn't say anything till he was ready to leave. He stopped in the doorway and turned.

"Well," he said, "this is where I came in. So long."

Dusty didn't get it, for a minute, and by the time he did Rick was halfway to his car. Dusty called to him, but he didn't turn, and Dusty let it go at that. There'd be plenty of time to make Rick see that the show wasn't over and that the best of it, for both of them, was still ahead. And meanwhile—he quit thinking about Rick. Jan was over by the old Pierce and she lifted her arm and waved it.

She shook her head when Dusty started to go around to the right side of the car.

"Not any more," she said. "You're driving now."

Dusty climbed in behind the big wheel. He was thinking that this was a better way of saying it than any of the things a woman had to say when she was getting married. But the only answer to it that he could think of was one of the things that a man said.

"And with all my worldly goods——"

Jan leaned against his arm.

"I knew it would be like that," she said. "I knew we weren't going to have to talk—much."

They didn't talk at all for a long while. Not till they were out on the concrete, coming toward a big filling-station at a cross-roads.

"Let's stop here," Jan said. "I want to call up Dad and tell him——" She sat up straight, laughing.

"Why, I don't know your name, do I? What is it?"

Dusty steered in toward the row of pumps.

"Well?" Jan said. "Why don't you tell me?"

"Because I wanted it to last this much longer," Dusty said, "and it'll be all over when I tell you. But I guess you've got to know. It's Enoch."

Jan shook her head, like a boxer trying to recover from a punch. She looked Dusty over, slowly and soberly. Then she laughed.

"Well, Enoch," she said, *"nevertheless!"*

She got out and went into the station.

16

"I GUESS that was a poor hunch I had, telling you to scrape the tar off your pan, huh?" Guthead said.

Jan laughed. "Yes. Only you picked the wrong man for me to work it on. You said——"

"You worked it on a right guy, anyhow," Guthead said. He squinted at Dusty, over by the new storage tank, talking to Jim Hafey. "This one's got what it takes. All of it."

Jan only nodded but there was a glow inside of her. Guthead and his kind were hard to fool, harder to please. Not that she needed to hear it, of course;

it was just good to know that his judgment on Dusty matched her own. Some of the glow died, though, when she turned her head to look at the car that was drumming over the plank road. It was near enough for her to recognize it as Rick Farren's car, and in spite of everything she hadn't quite learned not to be afraid when anything reminded her of Rick.

It wasn't Rick, though, who was in the car. Stella Conway got out of it. She had on a cartwheel hat and a white linen dress and she was being choosy about where she put down her white, strap-heel pumps, taking little steps, with plenty of hip in them, like a candidate, Jan thought, for Miss East Texas. Jan had a smile ready for her, though, and it was a real one. Stella gave it back to her, gathering Guthead's eyes in passing like somebody stringing beads.

"Dusty here?" she said.

Jan's guard went up a little.

"Over there," she said, nodding. Stella's eyes measured the distance and gauged the mud.

"I guess it's better this way," she said. "You're the one I've got to sell, anyway."

"What college do you want to go to?" Jan said.

Her guard was still up. Joking was one kind of defense.

"Rick's going down to Bayou Rouge this afternoon," Stella said. "I thought maybe it would interest Dusty to know it."

Jan had been ready for it.

"It wouldn't," she said. "Not the way you mean. Dusty's all through with that crazy racket, and Rick's got just as much reason for being through with it as Dusty has. If he hasn't sense enough to quit——"

"He hasn't," Stella said, "but that isn't why he's doing this job and doing it for half price. He's doing that because it was the only way to pry that piece of your lease out of Rogan, after he found out how Dusty felt about it. Dusty doesn't know about that. I thought maybe he ought to know it, before Rick goes up against that Bayou Rouge fire—alone."

"I don't understand," Jan said. It was queer, being so perfectly sure that Stella was telling the truth and yet not believing her. "Dan Rogan only bought the stock to——"

"Little Red Riding-Hood," Stella said. "Anything

with a lace cap on it is your grandma. All Dan Rogan was doing was to gather himself in another little lease. He already had Hafey's piece of this one and if Rick hadn't got that stock away from him, he'd have had control of your company. This well would be capped and there wouldn't be any more, and you could either say uncle or eat hay."

"I don't believe it," Jan said. "I know you think so, but you're wrong. Dan Rogan wouldn't——"

"Listen, Snowwhite. You've got instincts. Why don't you use them? If you found a dead fish in the road, would some grown-up have to tell you not to pat it? You can't tell me Dan Rogan doesn't give you goose-pimples. If you won't believe your own alarm-system, ask Guthead. He'll tell you."

"She's giving you the guy's right number, Jan," Guthead said. "Iced louse, Number One, net—that's him, for my money."

"Since when did you start pinning medals on him, Guthead?" Stella said. "Listen, Jan. Rogan's been trimming World Pete for years. Their scouts dig up something good and old Jim Hafey just happens to beat World Pete to it, and when World Pete buys him out it pays him plenty. But he's always broke, just the same. Why do you suppose that is?"

She waited. Jan didn't say anything. She wasn't sure yet, that it was true, but she was beginning to be sure.

Stella went on.

"It was a little different with this wildcat of yours. That was Hafey's own play. Rogan was dead sure there was no oil under here and didn't want any part of the bet—not till after it started looking good. Then he took over. If your well hadn't blown out it wouldn't be in now, and Rogan would own it, and plenty of other territory around here, too. You don't have to believe me. Ask Jim Hafey and he'll tell you. He's got his piece of your lease back, and he won't be taking Rogan's orders any more. He doesn't have to. Rogan used to have a sort of whip over him, but Rick cut the snapper off it."

She shook her head at Jan, something like the way a school-teacher might shake her head at a nice pupil who couldn't help being a little dumb.

"That's the lowdown, Jan. You don't believe it, but you know it. If it wasn't for Rick the only chance you'd ever stand of taking a dime out of this lease would be to marry Dan Rogan and prick your fingers, nights, on the fishhooks in his pocket. And Rick's going down to Bayou Rouge. It'll be up to you to say whether Dusty goes along. I'm not even going to wait here and put it up to him."

She did a Miss-East-Texas turn and went model-footing back to the car. Jan stood perfectly still.

"You could forget to tell him," Guthead said.

Jan shook her head. She knew he'd only said that to help her see that she had to tell.

"And you could tell him and still stop him from going," Guthead went on. "It'll come easy to him to yes you, after all the practice he's had yessing Rick."

"Go tell him I'm waiting for him in the car," Jan said. "Don't tell him why. Just say it's—just say it's something important."

She had a grip on herself by the time Dusty found her. She wasn't in the car, though, but only waiting near it. Being in it would be answering a question Dusty had to answer for himself.

She watched his face as she told him what Stella had told her. She knew what he was going to say but she didn't let him see how she was going to take it.

"I promised you I wouldn't——" he didn't get any farther than that. Jan waited, trying to keep her eyes from saying anything. He had to decide this himself.

"I can't help it, Jan. I've got to go."

"What are we waiting for?" Jan said.

His look told her, before his hands told her, that it was the right thing, the only thing, for her to say. And she didn't need the telling. She knew it was right, whatever happened.

Whatever happened. She kept pushing those two words out of her mind as the old car gave Dusty all it had. But they kept coming back. She was still fighting them off when they slid past the corner of the Beauregard-McGee and saw Rick's car in front of the gingerbread marquee. A flock of bellhops were elbowing each other to stow red-striped bags into the luggage compartment, and Rick and Stella were on the sidewalk, with Dan Rogan.

It was Rogan who saw the old Pierce first. His eyes—why hadn't she ever noticed before how pale they were?—drilled into Jan's. A dead fish, she thought. Her face must have told the eyes that she was thinking it. They didn't change, but there was something final about the way they shifted, sidling past her and away.

Rick was dealing out five-dollar bills to the bell-hops when he saw Dusty. He stopped, for a second, and then went on. Past his shoulder Jan saw Stella's face, and it was a little easier, suddenly, to fight off those two words because another woman was also trying, with everything she had, to push the same two away.

Dusty went over to Rick.

"What's the idea, Osage? You wouldn't be dumb enough to go after your gold spittoons alone, would you?"

"Well, look who's here!" Rick said. "The great big oil man, in person! This is certainly an honor, Mr. Rockefeller, coming to see me off, and don't think I don't appreciate it."

"See you off, hell!" Dusty said. "I'm coming with you."

"That's what you think," Rick said. Some of the deadpan look was gone, Jan noticed. "Your resignation's been accepted. Any time I go fooling around a fire the guy that goes with me won't be trying to look back over his shoulder. One swell way to stay in there is to be too anxious to get out. I'd sooner have Caspar Milquetoast back of me than you, Butch."

"You take me and like it," Dusty said. Rick grinned at him but he shook his head again.

"I'd be scared to, Butch. This is one business when a guy has to keep his mind right on his work and yours won't even get near it. That's why I might be quitting myself, after this job. The way I been changing ideas lately—" he angled a look at Stella—"I'm not any too sure where my own mind'll be—if any."

"That's swell," Dusty said. "We both quit, after we lick this one. But we lick this one together. That's that, Rick. You know it and you know why."

Rick took quite a while to think it over.

"Okay," he said. "That's that."

His eyes twisted to Jan.

"You win, Red, but I get one round. You couldn't keep him away, could you?"

"Keep me away?" Dusty said. "She brought me. I wouldn't even have known about it if she hadn't told me."

Jan watched Rick taking it. She had moved over to where Stella was standing. She did it without thinking, but there was a sort of rightness about being there, just as there had been the other day when they had watched Rick and Dusty walking toward the fire, just as there would be when they stood together, tomorrow, down at Bayou Rouge.

Rick came over to her.

"So I've got to change a few ideas about you, too, Red? Okay. They're changed." He looked sidewise at Dusty. "You may not be so hot about a lot of other things, Duss, but when it comes to picking partners—" he held out his hand and Jan's met it halfway—"when it comes to picking partners, you're terrific!"

END